Dearest
Ruth

FICTIONAL LIVES

with love

Hugh

16/12/13

Fictional Lives

HUGH FLEETWOOD

FABER & FABER

This edition first published in 2013
by Faber and Faber Ltd
Bloomsbury House, 74–77 Great Russell Street
London WC1B 3DA

Printed and bound by CPI Group (UK) Ltd, Croydon, CR0 4YY

A CIP record for this book is available from the British Library

ISBN 978–0–571–30479–0

For

Joe McCrindle

Contents

INTRODUCTION

On Beauty, and The Beast:
An Interview with Hugh Fleetwood

Hugh Fleetwood was born in Chichester, Sussex, in 1944. Aged twenty-one, he moved to Italy and lived there for fourteen years, during which time he exhibited his paintings and wrote a number of novels and story collections, originally published by Hamish Hamilton, beginning with A Painter of Flowers *(1972). His second novel,* The Girl Who Passed for Normal *(1973), won the John Llewellyn Rhys Memorial Prize. His fifth,* The Order of Death *(1977), was adapted into a 1983 film starring Harvey Keitel and John Lydon. In 1978 he published his first collection of short stories,* The Beast. *Subsequent collections have included* Fictional Lives *(1980) and* The Man Who Went Down With His Ship *(1988). He currently lives in London, and continues to work both as writer and painter.*

In this interview with Faber Finds editor Richard T. Kelly, recorded at the Faber offices in April 2013, Hugh Fleetwood discusses some of the key influences on his work, both from life and from art.

RICHARD T. KELLY: *Given the distinctive expatriate/Anglo-Italian dimension of your writing it does seem very significant that you moved away from England while still a young man. Was this a special ambition of yours?*

HUGH FLEETWOOD: Yes, I found England parochial, I hated the whole class business, absolutely loathed it – I still do. When I was seven years old I was sent to boarding school in Worthing, and we had an English master there who actually did say to us, 'You know, you boys are going to grow up to run the empire . . .' Even at that age, I thought, 'You are *insane*.' Then at thirteen I went to a public school, Eastbourne, which I hated with a passion – so much that it was the making of me, really. I was so determined to get away from the sorts of people I encountered there that I vowed I would leave the country as soon as I could.

There was a history teacher who loathed me – I don't know if it was personal, but one of my forebears had been a general under Cromwell and one of the many signatories of Charles I's death warrant. This teacher never forgave me for that. I remember writing in an essay something to the effect that Gladstone was the first English statesman to try to incorporate Christian morality into practical politics. He crossed this out and wrote, '*What about King Alfred?*' Alfred hadn't much figured in our syllabus, if he indeed existed. And at the bottom he added in red ink, '*But what can you expect from the descendant of a regicide?*'

RTK: *Weren't there any teachers who encouraged you in a creative direction?*

HF: I always painted, and there was one art teacher who thought I should go on to art school. But then he went off to America on an exchange, and his American counterpart didn't like me and I didn't like him, which put me off. But that was probably fortuitous . . . The school did have a painting competition, and I did a large oil of a black woman, naked, full frontal. They had to give me the first prize, it was the best entry, but they were terribly embarrassed. I was awarded £25 and a book of my choice, so I picked *Les Fleurs du Mal*. I think the general reaction was 'Typical Fleetwood' . . .

RTK: *What about literary interests? Were you reading much early? Did you write?*

HF: I started reading seriously, I suppose, when I was about 14

– Ibsen and Strindberg, and other names I would claim to have read, and then had to catch up on very quickly . . . But by the time I was sixteen, seventeen, I loved German literature and music, I was fascinated by that culture. These were the post-war years, of course, and it often seemed that the Germans were blamed for every sin throughout history. Obviously they were guilty to an extent. But I also felt the English weren't nearly so spotless as they purported to be. There was an awful lot of self-righteousness. I mean, history teaches us – we may be rich and civilised now, but we didn't get to be so by being nice, did we? We did it basically by killing people who were less rich and less quote-unquote civilised. We all know that and we all accept that.

RTK: *As Ernest Jones said of the British Empire, 'On its colonies the sun never sets but the blood never dries . . .'*

HF: Yes, and all empires have been the same. I'm sure when the Romans invaded Britain they were hated. But a thousand years go by and the account becomes rather more sanitised . . .

When I was sixteen or seventeen I started writing short stories, too, and then a novel – I knew it 'wouldn't do', but I did finish it. And as soon as I finished school I went to Paris for six months.

RTK: *Why Paris? Did you speak the language?*

HF: Only a little, but I'd been there with my parents and liked it; I had family in Paris who agreed to put me up. And Paris seemed the nearest place that was 'abroad' – it was just that lure of getting away. And I loved it. I was passionate about film, and Paris was wonderful for the cinema. I would go three times a day, it only cost one franc, and I got my film education that way, saw every old Hitchcock, Ford, Renoir, Von Sternberg . . . Eventually my parents said to me, 'Come back to England, go to university, at least until you're twenty-one, and if you still want to live abroad then go.' I always got on well with my parents – they both seemed very normal to me, and I suppose I must have seemed very un-normal to them, but they were extraordinarily tolerant. So I did as they asked. I started studying Law, detested it. All I remember is I sat in lectures next to Tim Rice. And the day after my twenty-first birthday I left the country and vowed never to return – a vow I didn't quite manage to keep . . . But when I went my parents said, 'It's your life, you're old enough to know what you want to do, we hope it works out.'

RTK: *How did you manage to arrange your escape?*

HF: I was sharing a flat in Lambeth and a girl in the flat worked for OUP. She introduced me to a German publisher based in Munich who told me that if I went to Munich and learned some German he'd give me some sort of job. So I went, but I wasn't happy – it was expensive, I could see my money running out in a fortnight, certainly before I'd learned enough German.

One day I went to the train station and saw there was a train leaving for Italy the following morning. I'd never been there, didn't speak a word of Italian, but I thought, 'What the hell, I can't go back to England . . .' The next morning – it was 8 a.m., 26 October 1965 – I got on that train. It was freezing cold, the taxi driver who drove me to the station was blowing on his fingers. But when I arrived in Florence at eight o'clock that evening it was still summer, and I'd never seen anything so beautiful. That was that . . .

I stayed in Florence for three months, learning Italian, but there were too many foreigners in Florence to teach English, and soon I was down to my last £1.50. So I hitchhiked to Rome with an American girl I'd met. She had a 'sort of' boyfriend there, and she said if she slept with him then he would put us up for a week. So I urged her to sacrifice herself . . . In Rome I thought the only thing I could do was teach English so I called at a language school. They didn't need anybody but they pointed me to another place down the road, and there the directress essentially asked me when I'd like to start. I said 'Now', and she said, 'I suppose you'll need an advance . . .?' She opened her handbag and gave me 80,000 lira, a month's salary, me having just walked in off the street. But I did a training course, and an American who started the same day as me had a room in a *pensione*, so I moved in there.

RTK: *And in Rome did you feel you had found the place you'd been searching for?*

HF: To begin with, I didn't like Rome as much as Florence. But by the time I had enough money to leave I didn't want to. Yes, I loved it. It was very easy as a foreigner, I had to get a *permesso di soggiorno* but the school did that for me. After that you paid no taxes, and there weren't so many of us foreigners about, so you met people. I made friends, got an apartment of my own, was very happy. Also I just felt, perhaps naively, that there weren't the same class divisions in Italy as in England. There were regional differences, people said they were from Tuscany or Naples or whatever, but not the stultifying class divisions you saw in England. As 'a foreigner', one was labelled to that degree, but not as any sort of class.

RTK: *Did the Rome of the mid-1960s still have the feel of la dolce vita?*

HF: It was the tail end of that, yes. I'd been there a year when a friend drove to visit me, his first time in Italy, and these were the days when the Via Veneto was still the place to meet. So I arranged to see him at the Café de Paris, the centre of civilised life at the time. You had to fight to get a table, always, but I fought and won one for us – next to a table that had been reserved, oddly. My friend joined me and sat down and two minutes later Luchino Visconti, Anna Magnani, and Raf Vallone came and took that reserved table. So I felt I'd organised it perfectly . . .

After 1968 things changed, then the Red Brigades stuff started, which changed the atmosphere of the place to some extent – not altogether. You became conscious of it, of bombs going off. But then bombs were going off in London too.

RTK: *How were your literary tastes developing in this time?*

HF: My great literary love at that time was Christopher Isherwood. When I went to Italy I couldn't take much luggage but I did take *Goodbye to Berlin*, which I would read from cover and cover, and then start again. Patricia Highsmith I loved, too. *The Blunderer* in particular I thought was wonderful. Like most people of that age I loved the Russians – Dostoyevsky, Chekhov's stories, Lermontov. Then I read Pushkin's *Queen of Spades* and Nabokov's *Laughter in the Dark*. *Queen of Spades* just struck me as a perfect story. There was an element of magic in it. And it wasn't English . . . But both the Pushkin and the Nabokov made a huge impression on me, and I thought, 'That's what I want to do . . .' I hadn't written since school but I started writing more short stories.

I couldn't see my way for a while, wasn't sure what kind of novel I would write. But then, I knew an English girl in Rome – I'd known her before, and she had an appalling mother. This girl came out to Rome, her mother followed, and this mother was all pink and white, apparently genteel, and absolutely *poisonous*. That gave me the basic materials for my first novel, *A Painter of Flowers*. The main character was an autobiographical element. But I suppose all my books have been autobiographical, to some extent. It's not conscious, it just happens.

I'd been teaching for four years when I got the news that *A Painter of Flowers* would be published. So I went to the language school and informed them that I'd never do another honest day's work in my life. And, touch wood, I never have . . . But they were very nice about it. The directress actually bought the painting of mine that was on the jacket of the novel.

RTK: *You were still painting as keenly as before?*

HF: Yes. I exhibited for the first time in 1970, in Spoleto, The Festival of Two Worlds. I knew a young American art dealer in Rome who liked my paintings. He called me, said, 'I'm having a small exhibition of a Spanish painter, would you like to have a joint exhibition?' I said, 'Who's the Spanish painter?' He said, 'Picasso.' I said, 'Yes.' I got a nice review in the *Herald Tribune*, from someone who'd presumably gone to see the Picassos . . . But for some time thereafter I really concentrated on the writing, still painting, but not so much.

I got the idea for my second novel through a friend of mine who was teaching a girl who had learning disabilities – teaching her, more or less, 'to be normal.' And the girl she was teaching had a mother who washed her hair in eggs, which her daughter apparently hated. So that was the seed for *The Girl Who Passed For Normal*, and the rest of the story came to me somehow . . .

RTK: *Did you find the storytelling part of novel-writing came easily? Or was it a lot of work to make all the elements fit together?*

HF: Plotting for me was always natural. It's usually just a small incident that forms itself into a whole story – like the proverbial grain of sand in the oyster, where the pearl forms around it. I work out the story on the back of an envelope, as it were, but I try not to think about it too much or else I find it becomes contrived. I've begun books where I've tried to plot too much in advance and then had to abandon them, because they haven't worked. I've tried never to analyse where the work comes from, because I'm afraid if I did then it would all disappear. The same with my painting – people ask me what a picture means and I say, 'I have no idea.' Someone once suggested to me, when I was being more than usually neurotic, that I should go see an analyst. I said, 'No, that would destroy any talent that I've got . . .'

RTK: *Do you think you're inclined by temperament toward 'dark' endings for your stories? Rather than, say, 'redemptive' ones?*

HF: Oh, I think most of them are redemptive in a way. People get what they want . . . Like Barbara in *The Girl Who Passed for Normal*, or like Wilbur in *An Artist and a Magician*. Originally I wanted to call that book 'A Tax On Added Value' but I was advised it wasn't a good title. Essentially, though, that is what the book is about. Value has been added to Wilbur's life but he has to pay a moral tax on it. You could say the same of *The Girl*.

RTK: *You say your characters 'get what they want'. But I sometimes find myself wondering how they would manage to go on with their lives after the last page.*

HF: Well, that's something we all have to deal with, isn't it?

RTK: *Earlier you mentioned Patricia Highsmith as an influence on your writing. Highsmith famously said that she was 'interested in the effect of guilt' upon the heroes of her stories. Do you think you are interested in something similar?*

HF: No – not 'guilt', that's not something I really recognise. I would say I'm interested in characters coming to terms with things, in themselves and in the world. It's about their arriving at a knowledge, of murder, of death . . . And then they use this, and grow out of what they were. That's a conscious theme of all my books.

RTK: *In your own life would you say you've had experiences that affected you in just this way?*

HF: I think for my generation a big part of it was growing up just after the war, in the shadow of that, which had a profound effect on me, certainly, and from an early age. I remember, at school, reading accounts of concentration camps. And you were told this was what the Germans were capable of – or the Russians, in the case of the gulags. But these things weren't dreadful because they were done by Russians or Germans. I thought, 'This is what *human beings* are capable of.' It led you to wonder how you would cope in that situation – cope, I mean, whether on one side or the other, whether one was in such a camp or running it.

The other main theme in my books, I suppose, is the 'beauty and the beast' element – that you have to have them both, you can't have one without the other. Beauty without the beast is shallow, meaningless.

RTK: *Would you say it's a necessary acknowledgement of evil in the world?*

HF: Not 'evil', just the facts of life. I don't really 'do' evil (*laughs*). I hate the word 'innocent', too – I know what people mean by it but I just don't buy it. There's ignorance and then there's knowledge, or there should be.

People say Francis Bacon's paintings are horrific, but I find them beautiful as paintings. The subject matter is, in a sense, irrelevant. If you consider the power of Renaissance painters who painted crucifixions – the subject may be tragic or whatever you want to call it, but if the paintings are beautiful then in that way you get the whole package. The Grunewald *Crucifixion* in Colmar, for example, is horrific but also beautiful. Whereas paintings by someone like Renoir who just did flowers and rosy-cheeked girls are much uglier to me.

RTK: *So the artist needs to make an accommodation with the horrific, to look at it squarely?*

HF: Oh, I think everybody should, artists or no. I should say, I don't think artists are any more corrupt than anyone else – I just think they should stop pretending that they're *less*.

A Wonderful Woman

SHE HEARD THE NEWS while working in the garden—Maisie just shouted it to her: 'Brandon's dead,'—and for a moment felt such a sense of triumph she thought she would faint. He was dead! He was gone. The only one who had ever worried her. The only one who had ever stood between her and peace. Gone, gone, gone . . . She was sorry of course—he was the same age as her, and fifty-three was too young to die—but nevertheless now she was free, and now nothing would ever be able to disturb her existence, her small old house on its Tuscan hillside, her large garden where she grew all her own food, and her relationship with Maisie. Now she was beyond recall. . . .

'How?' she shouted back, as Maisie got out of the car holding the newspaper, which she had just driven into the village to buy.

'In a motor accident.'

She was glad about that too, she thought, as she put the flower she'd been holding in a basket, and picked another. At least if he'd had to go it had been quick; it hadn't been cancer, or something long and lingering. She wouldn't have wished that on him.

'Where?' she called, more hesitantly now—suddenly afraid her friend might hear her joy.

For the third time Maisie's quiet voice came down the hill.

'In England.'

And then, at last, as she took this in, the sense of triumph left her, and she felt nothing but regret.

Regret that the only writer in the world she admired was

dead; regret that the only man in the world she admired was dead.

A month later Tina Courtland received a letter from her publisher.

She had driven into the village herself one morning—Maisie, whose task and pleasure it normally was to buy the paper, had a headache—and decided, once there, to pass by the post office, to see if there was any mail. She hadn't really been expecting any—she never did—and was surprised therefore when the plain pleasant girl behind the counter handed her an envelope with her name on. She was even more surprised when, having thanked the girl, she went out into the street, and started reading:

Dear Tina,

It has been a long time. I hope you and Maisie are well. Here things are very much as usual. I am writing because I have a proposal to put to you.

I expect you have heard that Joseph Brandon was killed in a car crash a few weeks ago. Naturally we were all very shocked, and literary considerations aside, it was a great personal loss to me.

Anyway, I have decided—both because we were his publishers for the last twenty-five years, and because it is needed —to commission a biography of him. I have discussed the matter with Margaret, his widow—she has all his personal papers, along with a number of unpublished stories etc.— and she is all in favour, on one condition.

Now Tina, I know you have written nothing for the last eight years, and swore, when you left London, that you would never write anything again. I am hoping to persuade you to change your mind. Because Margaret Brandon was quite categorical in stating that you were the only person she would trust to undertake the job, and said that Joe himself had often told her that if anything happened to him, if you weren't around—or weren't willing—to 'do' him, then no one else was to, and his papers were to be destroyed.

Of course I realize you only met Brandon once, and could not consider yourself a friend, or even an acquaintance. And you have apparently never met Margaret. But I cannot forget that he was the only colleague of yours you had any respect for, that you did write some remarkable pieces on him in the past for the *New York Review* and the *TLS*, and that you both, to a remarkable degree, had similar backgrounds. Both expatriate Americans, both raised as Catholics, and both from the South. (Yet neither of you 'Southern' or 'Catholic' writers.) Added to which—as must be obvious—*you* were the only fellow writer whom Brandon himself admired; and indeed only three months ago he asked me if I had heard from you, and said that your stopping writing had always seemed a tragedy to him.

So—what do you think? I realize that if you accept this commission it will involve your coming to London, and possibly returning to the States; neither of which is likely to please you. Nevertheless, I would beg you to give the matter your most serious consideration. For (apart from the fact that Margaret seems quite serious in her intention to destroy the papers if you don't accept) I am convinced that only you could do full justice to Joe Brandon—and even more convinced that only you, while doing full justice to him, could write a book that is, if you'll excuse the expression, a work of art in its own right.

I look forward to hearing from you. My best regards to Maisie and yourself, As ever, Christopher.

Tina's first reaction, once she had finished this—and once she had recovered from her surprise—was, of course, to dismiss the idea as preposterous, and forget all about it. She write a biography indeed! Her second reaction however—that came to her as she strode through the narrow streets back to the car —was that she should discuss the matter with Maisie. For while she was naturally tempted to act on impulse, and justify that impulse later, Maisie was not only far more cautious, but also, she had come to believe over the last eight years, of rather sounder judgement than herself.

Not, in this case, that she doubted what her friend would say.

She was wrong though. Maisie, that evening, advised acceptance.

'It'll do you good to get away,' she said. 'You've been cooped up here too long.'

They were sitting in their small book-lined living room; and Tina felt tears come into her eyes.

'I can't possibly leave,' she protested. 'Apart from anything else, who would take care of everything?'

'Who do you think?' Maisie smiled. 'I'm quite capable, you know.'

'Yes, of course I know. Only—'

Only she didn't like to admit it. One of the understandings of their life together was that she, so tall and square, with her crop of blonde hair, was the strong one, the one who looked after the physical side of things; while quiet, pale, sandy-coloured Maisie, who was ten years her senior, who didn't like to go out in the summer because of the insects, and who spent most of her life behind netting, was good only for buying newspapers, doing accounts, and—at a pinch—feeding cats and dogs. This did overlook the fact that Maisie had spent twenty years of her life working as a doctor in the slums of Bombay, whereas until they had moved here Tina Courtland

4

had never done anything more practical than buy cut flowers and lift a pen to paper. But somehow—

'And it's not as if we don't have help here, or that you'd be away for long. You'd only have to go to London for a couple of months probably. Talk to the wife and friends, make copies of any letters or papers you think are relevant. Then you can come back here and work in peace.'

'But I don't want to work. I've said all I have to say, between us we're all right for money, and anyway, I don't like London.'

'You do. You've just convinced yourself you don't. Besides,' Maisie added, 'you should do it because you envied Brandon.'

'I did not.'

Maisie smiled, and picked up the book she'd been reading.

'I didn't, really,' Tina insisted. And she hadn't, she told herself. She had simply believed that he was the one man who seemed capable of writing something that wasn't totally false, that wasn't totally compromised, and had thought that if her belief were correct—if someone, anyone could write a book that wasn't untrue—then it might have been possible for her to continue writing. But she had also thought that her belief probably wasn't correct; just that she was incapable of detecting the fundamental dishonesty of Brandon's work.

'Well anyway,' Maisie murmured after a while, 'I still think you should do it. I mean I know it'll be difficult for you. But if the man did trouble you, you should try to find out why. Even if he's dead now.' She looked up. 'You never know, you might suddenly find you want to write another novel yourself.'

'Never,' Tina said firmly, getting to her feet. But she sounded firmer than she felt. For she had to admit that, as so often, Maisie did have a point. Brandon *had* troubled her; and if she could only find that dishonesty in him she was sure must exist, there would be no danger that, in another five or ten years, she would repent of her decision to have abandoned her career. While if she didn't find it, or didn't even look for it, though she had felt so triumphant when she had heard the news of his death, that danger would always exist.

It would be appalling, she thought, as she went over to the window and gazed, through the June evening, over her fruit trees and vines, if she ever did come to repent of all this; repent of her having more or less forced Maisie to give up her job; repent of their having moved to Italy (that also had been her idea); repent of their not having stayed on in London, she locked up in her study, and Maisie working at the hospital, doing her research into tropical medicine.

'But how,' she asked plaintively—and it was to be her last word on the subject that evening—'will I be able to face it?'

'Oh Tina,' Maisie laughed quietly from her book, 'I told you. You don't dislike the outside world as much as you've convinced yourself you do. And you're just as capable of facing life in London as I am of watering the plants, cooking, and making sure Giovanni does whatever it is he does. After all,' she concluded, 'you faced it for long enough, and you were quite successful at it.'

Yes, Tina thought, six weeks later in England: that was so. But it was in the past. Whereas today, sitting in the office Christopher had put at her disposal, looking down at Long Acre, and watching the cars and people move along the street, she really wasn't sure if she could face it any longer. It was all so ugly, so squalid, so tedious. . . . Not that she had anything against London in particular; in fact it had always been her favourite city, as far as cities went. But to think that this was reckoned one of the centres of civilization! Oh certainly the majority of those people walking down there did the best they could, and she didn't for a minute imagine she was in any way superior to them. After all—as Maisie had said—she herself, until eight years ago, had been one of them, and had been

6

hailed as a success by them, and by the city—the world—in which they lived. As, on their terms, she had been. But—what terms! She had only done it, she thought, in order to be able to dismiss success; to be able to know, having tasted the fruit, that she didn't like its flavour. And now, now that she did know, to have come back! To have abandoned her refuge up on that Italian hill. To have returned to face not just the fact that, however loathe she was to admit it, her being there depended on all this being here, but also, and worse, the fact that ugly, squalid and tedious though she did find it, it was undoubtedly far better, in terms of justice and freedom and health, than it had ever been. She had been mad!

But it was all, she allowed herself to whisper, as she continued to gaze from the window, the fault of men. . . .

She hated men with a passion that she knew was unreasonable—for apart from anything else she was doubtful that if women ruled and always had ruled the world, things would be so very different—and with a passion that she generally tried to keep in check. But at times—and this was one of them—she had, if she weren't to explode, to indulge herself. And so, for the next fifteen minutes now, she allowed herself to be swept away by her feelings of revulsion. Her revulsion for the way men looked, her revulsion for the way men smelled, her revulsion for the attitudes of men, and above all, her revulsion for the world that they had made. Because it was all very well to tell herself that women might not have done a better job, but the point was they had never had a chance to. And who knows if she might not be wrong. If, if women had made the rules, this whole planet might not have been an infinitely kinder, fairer, and more beautiful place. . . .

At the end of fifteen minutes, however, her fever started to abate; and after another five minutes she even went so far as to dwell on the possibility that this flare-up of her condition had been caused not by any sudden realization of how much

7

she despised men and the world that they had made (after all, she had known that for forty years), but, at this particular moment, by the sudden realization that so far she had found nothing, absolutely nothing, to hold against Joseph Brandon.

She had been here for a week, and had already spoken, in interviews that had been arranged for her by Christopher, to most of Brandon's friends and colleagues in London. She had read through as many letters, both from him and to him, as she and Christopher had been able to lay their hands on. She had read two early unpublished novels, and four short stories, that Margaret Brandon had sent round. And she had read the proofs of a book of memoirs about growing up in the South that Brandon had finished shortly before his death. (A book that, taken in conjunction with *her* memories of growing up in the South, she had decided made it unnecessary for her to return to Alabama.) Yet from all this material there had, so far, emerged only the portrait of a man that matched in almost every detail the image she had formed of him when she had met him that one time years and years ago—on his very first day in London, in fact.

The image of a large, bear-like, good-humoured man, unpretentious, extraordinarily intelligent, and radiating what she could only think of as an overwhelming integrity. A man whose love of life was all the more genuine for his being aware of the horrors of life.

Yet there had to be some detail she had overlooked. There had to be, she told herself as she sat there at her desk. Because if it *were* possible to continue living in this world (and, incidentally, writing books) without being dishonest, she might indeed repent of her decision to retire.

Oh, she thought, she should have trusted her instinct when she had received Christopher's letter. She *should* have dismissed the idea as preposterous, never have mentioned the matter to Maisie, and clung to her belief that she just wasn't capable of seeing through Joseph Brandon. For really if she didn't manage to see through him now, knock him, as it were, down, there would be no alternative for her but to return to the world, and to resume her career. And she didn't want to. She was happy in Italy, growing her vegetables and making her own wine. She was happy up there on her hill with Maisie, and—but was Maisie happy, she suddenly wondered. Could Maisie have persuaded her to do this book because she hoped it would cause them to return to London? Did she miss the city and the theatres, the music and their friends? No, she told herself. No, it wasn't possible, and of course Maisie was happy. If she hadn't been she would have said so. Maisie was not one to suffer in silence. No—she had simply believed, as she had said, that it would be good for her friend to get away, for her to write one more book to make sure she didn't regret her having given up everything, and for her to lay, once and for all, the ghost of Joseph Brandon; that ghost who threatened to drag her back into the world.

What Maisie hadn't presumably foreseen was that that ghost could not be laid; and that it would go on beckoning and beckoning, whispering 'there is a way', until Tina Courtland followed. . . .

Still, she told herself finally, she did have one more chance. She hadn't, yet, met Margaret Brandon—who had been away in the country since she had arrived, and with whom she had an appointment tomorrow morning. Perhaps Margaret Brandon would tell her something she hadn't known; tell her that thing she wanted to know. Perhaps Margaret Brandon would provide her with the means to exorcise her devil. . . .

What kind of means she wasn't certain, and really, when she went to Chester Street at eleven o'clock next day, she held no great hopes that this last and most important interview would help her any more than the others had. But a minute after she had been let into the house, and was talking to the woman, her spirits started to rise at last. Not because she believed, having met her, that Mrs Brandon would tell her anything she didn't already know, but because she immediately felt that the woman herself might be the clue she had been searching for.

She was all wrong. Wrong, according to Tina, in a general way, and wrong, especially, as the wife of Joseph Brandon. She didn't fit into the portrait, as it had been painted so far, in any way. Tina had heard that she had been a dancer before she had married the writer, and was the daughter of an English father, who had been a diplomat, and an Austrian mother. She had been expecting someone bright, practical, perhaps not too intelligent, with a few rather carelessly worn remnants of a former prettiness. What she was confronted with was a bleak, freezingly beautiful woman in her late forties, who seemed to have just stepped out of the pages of some fashion magazine. She had blonde hair that was cut with elaborate simplicity. She had a face that was as stretched and painted as a canvas. She had a body that was slim as a seventeen-year-old girl's. And she wore a beige silk dress, beige high-heeled shoes, and a single gold chain around her neck that were almost parodies of elegance. As a dummy she would have been wonderful; as a person she was terrifying. There was nothing natural about her; nothing. Not the way she spoke— in a low, soft, expressionless voice—not the way she moved—as if performing in a drawing-room comedy—not even the way she looked; with eyes that, instead of noting, with amusement or disdain, the contrast between herself and the tall, broad-shouldered, blue-trousered and blue-shirted woman facing her, gazed emptily into space. She was the sort of woman whom Tina always wanted to grab and shake until she fell to bits; or whom she wanted to grab and kiss, until the man-made façade collapsed, and revealed a woman who, precisely because she was so man-made, was in the most profound despair, and was only longing to be released from the hell in which she lived. But though, once or twice, when she had been younger, she had done just this (and on one occasion actually had released, as she liked to think, the woman within) now she was too old or too tired to contemplate such a move. And so, having taken note of her desire, she simply concentrated on the task in hand; which was first to try to understand how, knowing what she knew of him, and of his work, a man like Joseph Brandon could have married a creature like this; and second, to try to see the way she could use Margaret Brandon as a pin with which to bore through the castle wall of her late husband's impregnability.

She concentrated for an hour, which was as long as the interview lasted. She concentrated while Margaret Brandon offered her coffee, while Margaret Brandon, in her expression-less voice, said all the things that everyone else had said about Joseph Brandon—that he was a man of great integrity and good humour, that he was a man who believed (though he never said so as such; he disliked making grand statements) that art alone could tell the truth about the world, could reconcile man to the miseries of existence, and reveal to man the wonders of existence, and that he was a man who believed that the great, the only important thing was to *live*—and she concentrated while Margaret Brandon took her to the study where her husband had worked, and showed her round the house. (Which, so shocked had Tina been before, she had hardly noticed till now; but which, when she did take it in, shocked her almost as much as its mistress, to which it was, in its way, similar. A beige, beautifully furnished, very elegant and utterly lifeless place that wouldn't do at all as a back-ground to the image she had already formed of Joseph Brandon). But concentrate though she did, feel steadily more certain though she did that Mrs Brandon was the proof of something rotten in the writer, and feel correspondingly ever more relieved that she had at last found some proof, by the time she left the house she had still neither understood, nor seen in what way she could make use of her finding.

There was something more she had to learn, she told herself as she walked slowly through the hot dusty streets towards her hotel. She had seen in Margaret Brandon the symptoms of a disease. Now she had to discover the nature of the disease itself. To discover it, and label it—and thus make sure that her present conviction that Joseph Brandon had indeed been rotten didn't slowly fade away; leaving her only with the suspicion that her reaction to his widow had been nothing more than some mixture of jealousy and resentment, and a priggish feeling that it was unsuitable for a great and famous author to be married to a doll, and live in luxury better suited to a banker.

Which wasn't true, she thought, as she reached her hotel. There *had* been a flaw in Brandon, and she *would* find out what it had been; and she would set it down in her book for all the world to read. And then she would be safe forever.

She had had to wait for years to get this far; she only had to wait one more day to reach her destination.

Before she did, however, she learned something else which affected her profoundly; something which Christopher revealed to her when he came into her office the following morning.

'What,' the publisher said, 'did you make of Margaret?'

Tina looked at the tall thin man—of whom she was, in spite of his sex, very fond—and wondered whether he was a friend of the widow, and whether she should be diplomatic. But never having been one for diplomacy, and in any case catching a note in Christopher's voice which suggested that he didn't make very much of her himself, she shrugged and said, 'I thought she was one of the most appalling people I have ever met in my life.'

Christopher laughed. 'I guessed you might not approve.' He paused, and glanced briefly at his hands. 'Though it's a shame you never met her when she was younger, before they were married. She was quite different then. I think you would have liked her then.'

'Different how?'

'Oh, fatter—well anyway plumper—more of a mess, more fun, more natural, more lively, and—' he paused again, and smiled shyly, 'I don't know whether you'll approve of me saying this, but if she's beautiful today, in a rather scary way, she was *pretty* when she was young.'

Tina now laughed. 'Really,' she said, 'I have nothing against pretty women.'

She laughed, and she appeared to take Christopher's comments lightly. But within, this revelation made her tremble. Margaret Brandon *had* once been as she had imagined that she would be. So Brandon hadn't married a monster; he had *created* a monster. Oh, it was terrible, she thought; and made her all the more determined to expose the man.

'And the house?' she said. 'I thought that was pretty awful, too.'

Again Christopher smiled shyly. 'I'm afraid that was Joe's doing as well. He bought it when he first started making a lot of money. He told me that when he'd been a boy he'd seen a photograph of Chester Street, and had thought that one day he would like to live there. He had a thing about eighteenth-century elegance. I could never see how it fitted in with the rest of his character.' He nodded at Tina, and smiled for the last time. 'I'm hoping that's what you're going to explain to us all.'

'I will if I can,' Tina said with passion. 'Don't worry about that.'

'I never worry about you,' her publisher murmured—and then held out a bulky package he'd been carrying. 'I don't know if these will help you at all. Margaret rang up yesterday after you'd left her and said she'd forgotten to give them to you. She found them after Joe's death. They're diaries or something, apparently. I sent a messenger round for them.'

'Have you read them?' Tina asked, more than ever trying to appear calm, and more than ever trembling within; trembling now with the sense—with the certainty—that here, in this brown paper package, she would find what she wanted to know.

'Me?' Christopher seemed shocked. 'Good heavens, no. I don't want to poach on your territory.' He looked at his watch. 'But I must leave you now. I have a meeting at ten-thirty.' He laid the package on the desk. 'Happy reading.'

'Thank you,' Tina said, still making an effort to appear unconcerned.

'Oh, and while I remember.' Christopher paused at the door. 'Pat said to ask you if you could come to dinner with us next Tuesday—today week.'

'Thank you,' Tina said again, only wishing at the moment that the man would go, so she could open that package. 'I'd like that.'

And she would have liked it, for she was as fond of Christopher's wife as she was of him. But she didn't go to dinner the following Tuesday. In fact she returned to Italy that very evening.

Inside the package were three large notebooks.

On the corner of one was written 1953–1963; on the corner of the second 1963–1973; on the corner of the third 1973——.

She started at the beginning.

June 24, 1953.
Yesterday I arrived in London for the first time and im-

14

mediately if absurdly felt I had come home. I also decided, as I stepped off the plane, that I would in future keep a sort of diary. I say a sort because my novels, I guess, are my real diary. But here I shall keep a record of the undigested facts of my life; or the undigestible facts.
So—here goes.

There followed a brief passage of Brandon's first impression of the city; which Tina skimmed through quickly. For even as she had read these opening words, her eye had been caught by something further down that first page.

In the evening Dick, and a young editor called Christopher something (I didn't catch his name), took me to dinner in an Italian restaurant. We were joined by two compatriots of mine: Charles McDonald, a pompous old fool who didn't impress me one bit, in spite of his reputation; and a fellow Southerner, Tina Courtland, whose book I haven't read yet but who impressed me greatly. She is a tall, solid girl of around twenty-five, I'd guess, with a handsome man's face, crew-cut blonde hair, an earnest manner and a voice that tends to get weepy when she becomes intense—which is often. She is clearly unaffected by the success that first novel of hers has had, and even seems scornful of it. She was also unaffected and seemingly scornful of Dick's attempts to be 'gentlemanly' with her. But I'm not a gentleman so we got on well—at least until the end of the dinner.

They had got on well; and Tina clearly remembered that evening, and the young Alabaman she was never to meet again. His grey eyes that were too cool for his warm manner, had, when they caught hers, acknowledged a kind of kinship with her; and his tall solid body and handsome man's face, that had made both Dick and Christopher seem very slight, and shadowy, had made her feel that she had found, in him, a twin.

I guess by then we had both drunk too much, and I was also tired after my flight. Anyway, we started getting aggressive with each other, and also, as one tends to when drunk and tired, started making deep pronouncements about life and art etc. etc. First of all we just sort of sparred with each other—but then when Tina C. solemnly stated, in her weepiest voice, that 'The history of the world is the history of crime, and the writer's task as I see it is to denounce crime', the fun really started. (Dick gave us both a look that implied we were country folk going on about country matters.) To begin with I laughed, then I knocked over my glass, and then I made *my* solemn statement. Which was (more or less): 'You may be right about the history of the world being the history of crime, but if you are, the writer's task as *I* see it is to celebrate crime. Without crime there would be no progress, there would be no justice, there would certainly be no art, there would, paradoxically, be no *check* on crime, and above all the human race would no longer exist.' At which Dick murmured 'Oh come now', Christopher looked amused, and Tina began to scream. She accused me of being a fool, she accused me of hating life, she accused me of every goddam thing she could think of, and finally she accused me of being a man. And when I murmured in my pleasantest fashion that I guessed as a woman she dissociated herself from history—and not only from history, but also from reality—because if she didn't she must certainly be a party to crime, she burst into tears, told me, yes, dissociate herself from history and reality was exactly what she did, because they were *man's* history and reality, gave me a look which proved she didn't believe what she said, and then ran out

16

of the restaurant so fast she knocked over a little old waiter who I'm sure still doesn't know what hit him.

Well, I guess I won't be seeing her again, though I'm sorry, because I did like her, and would like to continue my argument with her. That is get her to admit that she's wrong and I'm right. Which, fifteen hours and a good sleep later, I know I am. Denounce crime, my ass! Maybe I put it wrong when I said I reckon a writer should celebrate crime. Maybe what I should have said is that if her original premise is correct (which I think it is, though it depends on the angle you view things from; you could put it the other way round, and say the history of the world is the history of man's struggle *against* crime), and if therefore we are all a party to crime (because of course, as she virtually acknowledged with that look she gave me, she doesn't think for a moment that even if she is a woman she can dissociate herself from history and reality; though if she doesn't acknowledge it *openly* she'll end up retiring to the countryside with some girl-friend, raising chickens and growing vegetables instead of writing books), the writer's task is to describe the state of history and reality as it is now—to be in fact historians of the present—and let readers draw their own conclusions.

What I also should have said, I guess, is that if, once again, it is true that the history of the world is the history of crime, and we are all therefore parties to crime, it is the writer's task, the writer's duty—if he is to be an accurate historian—to know what he is writing about. To be, in other words, a criminal. To do willingly and consciously—not just, as is normal, unwillingly and unconsciously—what he believes to be wrong. If I can't write about love, if I have never loved—and I can't—I can't, by the same token, write about murder if I have never murdered. And I defy anyone to name a great work of literature that doesn't deal with either love or murder; generally both. By that I am not claiming that every great writer of the past has killed someone; but I am claiming that some (whether in war or by 'accident') have, that those who have not have missed the ultimate greatness they are capable of (the greatness that comes from knowing every corner of themselves, of the world, of life and death; the greatness of taking the whole world in and creating it anew; and the greatness to which I aspire, and which for me is the reason I want to live and write—ah to *be* the world, to be God—how else could I bear my existence!), and above all that I myself, while I have every intention of being 'good' (indulging in my love of life) have also every intention of being 'wicked'. (Indulging in my love of death.) Even up to and including murdering someone. For—to use a rather banal image—the love of life and the love of death are the twin motors on the ship of existence, and while I am here I wish to travel as far as I possibly can on that ship in exploration of the earth. To explore it, as I say, in order to re-create (no goddam it—*create*) it.

There, Tina Courtland! As we used to say—put that in your pipe and smoke it!'

Tina laid the notebook down and now, more than just trembling within, felt that her whole body was shaking. Not because she was embarrassed or upset by her recollection of the way that evening, all those years ago, had ended (lots of evenings had ended in a similar fashion when she had been young, and her fight with Brandon had in no way affected the impression she had received of him earlier that night), nor because these words she had read seemed to be a voice, literally from beyond the grave, that was speaking personally to her. Nor even—taken by themselves—because of the rantings about murder. She had heard others saying similar things, and generally understood them to be the longings of people, as writers often were, who felt themselves to be mere observers of life, mere sitters on the bank, and who yearned for some more active involvement in the world; some chance of being down there in the stream, swimming with everyone else.

No, what really made her shake was a combination of joy, and, unexpectedly, an almost hysterical fear. The joy was occasioned by her now even greater certainty that if she read on she would indeed reach her destination; would indeed discover the nature of Joseph Brandon's disease; would indeed be able to cast him out. The fear was occasioned by a premonition that in reaching that destination she was going to have to travel much further than she had ever wanted to go; that her discovery would not be—as she had always, when she had vaguely thought about it, imagined it would be—of some essentially minor ailment (some chronic eczema, as it were, of Brandon's soul) but of a disease so horrible, so contagious, that her very contact with it would put her in mortal danger; and that far from being able to cast out the carrier of this disease, she would find herself forced into isolation with him, without the possibility of feeling any joy whatsoever.

Such a premonition could, she thought, have been dismissed as pure fancy on her part (she didn't really think Brandon had gone round mugging old women, raping little girls, stabbing people for fun, did she?), if it weren't for two pieces of evidence she already had. One was the undisputed, well-publicized fact that throughout his life, though he had been based in England since 1953, Brandon had travelled continually; and travelled, more often than not, to countries in the grip of war or revolution. South America, Africa, the Far East—he had spent time in all these places, and even if friends, colleagues, and newspaper reports hadn't told Tina exactly when and where, she would have been able to tell from the novels; nearly all of which had wars and revolutions as their backgrounds, and nearly all of which, in one way or another, described the effect of the horrors of war and revolution on some uncommitted observer; or on someone who found himself in their midst by accident; or once—in the last, most successful, and in Tina's mind best book—on someone who had gone to a theatre of war (the Lebanon, in this instance) ostensibly in order to write articles condemning the conflict, but in fact because possessed by a lust for horror. . . .

There were passages in two or three of the books where the uncommitted observer, at the instant of realizing he could remain uncommitted no longer, found himself obliged to per- petrate the very crimes he had come to believe he must fight against; and in that book set in the Lebanon, a passage where the blood-hungry journalist is obliged to gratify his lust; and is destroyed in part by his at last first-hand knowledge of the nature of horror, and in part by his awareness that, even though he now entirely understands it and abhors it, he is more than ever consumed by a love of horror. . . .

Critics had always praised Brandon's perception, his 'deep insight into human psychology.' But what, Tina now thought, if that perception, that insight, had been achieved by the per- petration, *by Brandon himself*, of the crimes he pinned on his characters. She knew, after all, that in many instances he had befriended revolutionaries, and been in the front line of battles. He had always claimed, in the interviews she had read, that he had never once carried a gun, or gone into any of those battles armed. He had always gone strictly as an observer. But what if, what if. . . .

The second piece of evidence that made her think her pre- monition was justified, and that she would read things in those notebooks she didn't after all want to read—a piece of evidence she had already realized was significant, but now, in the light of what Christopher had said, became doubly so—was, of course, Margaret Brandon herself.

Because since everyone had insisted—and she had read a great many letters which substantiated these reports—that the couple had always gotten on extremely well, there was nothing to suggest that the writer had ever mistreated his wife. Nor was there much likelihood that they had been sexually incompatible; some of those letters had been quite explicit, and Margaret, yesterday, in her soft expressionless voice, had mentioned—in the same tone she had used to describe the provenance of some of their furniture—that she supposed one of the most difficult things for her to accept in Joe's sudden death was that she had been deprived not only of a husband, but also of a lover. So, if Brandon had not mistreated her, if she had been satisfied sexually, what *had* transformed Margaret from a plump, lively and pretty girl into the taut frozen object that she was today? Not finding herself married to a world-famous author, surely. Nor even finding herself with money—because she had also mentioned that her family had been reasonably well off. So, what then?

Ah, Tina thought, what but knowledge could have wrought such a change. And not knowledge of something unimportant. Knowledge of something too dreadful to know. Knowledge of the character of the man she was married to, and presumably loved. Knowledge of the character, if not of the deeds, that would be revealed by these notebooks.

She stared at them now, as they lay on the desk before her, and for a while was tempted to throw them in the waste-paper basket; or better, to go out, borrow a match from one of the secretaries in the building, and set fire to them.

But after a few minutes, and after having done something she hadn't done for eight years—which was smoke a cigarette; she went up to Christopher's office to beg one from him, saying that she had remembered she couldn't write without smoking—she had relaxed enough to realize that, even if she didn't read all the notebooks, she must at least read enough to be sure that she wasn't simply indulging in fantasies; that she did have reason to fear.

It took her another hour though to summon up the courage actually to do it; actually to expose herself.

She opened the second volume; and flicked through it until she saw a heading marked 'Congo'.

She read that for ten minutes; then she opened the third volume and read under the heading marked 'Vietnam'.

Fifty minutes later, still so white—she caught sight of herself in a mirror—she looked like a ghost, still unable to hear the traffic or the clacking of typewriters, and still so rigid with shock —a shock that was all the greater for being caused by something she had expected to happen—that she felt she was tearing her muscles with every step she took, she went once again to Christopher's office. But this time, instead of asking him for a cigarette, she told him shortly that Maisie had just phoned and said she had had a fall, that she was very sorry but she must return to Italy immediately, and that she had gathered, she believed, quite enough material to be getting on with. She would start work on the book itself soon, she said, would keep him informed as to her progress, and would return to London at a later date if she found it necessary.

And then, after she had brushed aside, with more briskness than she intended, Christopher's offers of assistance—'or at least a glass of brandy'—she returned briefly to her own office, picked up her large shoulder bag, picked up a larger bag containing all her notes, all Brandon's letters and papers, and the three volumes of diaries, and left the building; only pausing by the reception desk long enough to leave a message for Christopher that he should send her, as soon as possible, all Brandon's published work, and that she was, once again, sorry.

She took a taxi to the Alitalia offices and booked herself a seat on a flight to Pisa; she returned to her hotel and told the reception clerk she would be leaving that evening. And finally she went to her room and sat there; waiting. . . .

She waited for four hours; during which she read and re-read in her mind those pages of Joseph Brandon's diaries, realized that she had been right in thinking that, having read them, it would be impossible for her to feel any joy at all, and told herself over and over again that while, God knows, she had already learned far too much about the man—much much more than she had ever hoped or feared she would learn about him—she was well aware that what she *had* learned was but the tip of a colossal iceberg, and that if she were to pick up the notebooks again and read them all the way through, she would discover such a quantity of horror, such a depth of horror, that it would make what she had discovered so far seem almost trivial. At the end of four hours, though it wasn't time for her plane, she took the underground to the airport.

Because she couldn't help feeling that unless she did make a move right then, she might never be able to go home.

She remained in a state of shock for a week; telling a first concerned, and then really worried Maisie, that London had proved too much for her. But at the end of a week, assisted by the familiarity of her small and comfortable little house, by the warm, wonderful late September weather, by the necessity of having to take off Maisie's hands the details of the approaching grape-picking, and above all by Maisie's presence, and the renewed realization of how much she loved, and was loved by, her gentle, sandy-coloured friend, she started to pull herself together; started to prepare herself for the decision she knew must be made.

And three days later she was ready.

She had, she thought, four choices.

One was to write to Christopher, tell him that she couldn't

23

do the book, and send him back all the material she had—including the diaries.

The second was to tell Christopher that she couldn't do the book, and send him back everything except the diaries.

The third was to write a full exposure of Joseph Brandon; an exposure based upon the diaries, and an exposure that would cause a sensation.

And the last was to destroy the diaries, pretend she had never seen them, and write a biography that was, in effect, a work of fiction.

She went through them all in turn.

The first she had to reject because though in a way it would be the easiest thing to do, she was convinced (a) that if she didn't undertake the task Margaret Brandon wouldn't, as she had stated, and because of her husband's instructions, allow anyone else to, (b) that the woman's handing over to her of the notebooks had been a saying, in essence, 'Here, they're your responsibility; I don't know what to do with them,' and it was the least she could do for the poor abused creature to accept this responsibility, and (c) that in view of that message at the start of those notebooks, addressed personally to her, she was somehow bound to make the decision regarding their eventual publication or otherwise.

The idea of returning to Christopher all the material except the diaries she had to reject for the same reasons.

Which left her with just two alternatives: to reveal, or not to reveal. . . .

If only, she told herself (she was watering the garden at the time), she could have asked Maisie for advice. But she couldn't, she realized. Partly because if she had deferred to Maisie's judgement on most matters since she had given up her career, now she felt she *had* to make up her own mind and trust her instinct; and partly because if she did tell Maisie, she knew what her friend would say: 'Publish and be damned.'

Which, she finally admitted to herself, as she gazed towards the setting sun—and thus, almost by default, reached her decision—she didn't want to do. Neither publish, nor be damned. And while, in a way, she knew she should reveal the facts of Brandon's life (for deep down she still believed what she had so solemnly declared all those years ago: that it was the writer's task to denounce crime), she also knew that if she did force herself to read through those diaries, if she were to reveal to herself—let alone to the world—the full horror of the man (a horror she was more than ever sure she had glimpsed but a fraction of) she would indeed be damned. For aside from the scandal the book would cause—a scandal that would inevitably drag her back into the world—what she would learn would even more inevitably drag her, drive her back to the world. She would, by her very indignation, by her very feeling of outrage, and above all by the sense that her life itself, and her love of Maisie, were threatened, be forced out of retirement; be forced once again, and then again and again, to take up her pen, and write.

And she *couldn't* go through all that again, she nearly cried out loud. All right, she would admit that it was weak of her, wrong of her. She would admit that one couldn't, as long as one lived, retire. She would admit that she was dishonest in trying to dissociate herself from history, from reality—for of course women *were* just as responsible as men for the state of that history, for the state of that reality. She would even admit that her life here with Maisie was, in a way, a fiction, a pretended withdrawal from something that couldn't be withdrawn from. She would admit anything you like—but she would not go back to the world. For she did find it ugly and squalid and tedious; and would find it so much more ugly and squalid if

25

she were to return to it via Joseph Brandon's notebooks, that it would, she was sure, destroy her.

Oh, she thought: that she had never admired that man. Or at least that Margaret Brandon had never given her those notebooks.

But as she said the woman's name to herself, and started to walk slowly back to the house, she couldn't help wondering if the decision she had taken—taken, ultimately, to save herself —was the one Margaret Brandon had wanted her to take; and what, in the end, the woman would make of that decision.

Well, she told herself: she would see.

See she did; though not till two years had passed.

In the first seven months of those two years Tina wrote, at great speed and with remarkably little effort—it was just a chore she had to complete—what she had come to think of as her novel. A novel of which the prinicpal character was an adventurous, spirited young man who had grown up in the backwoods of Alabama, who had become an adventurous world-famous author, who—in the words of some dean of a college in Michigan, when conferring upon him an honorary degree—had 'told of the world as it is, and had shown that it is possible to live in this world with courage, nobility, grace and integrity', and who was, frankly, the sort of person his creator would have wished to be if she had been born a man.

In the following fourteen months she saw her book go into proof, be publicized by a very enthusiastic Christopher, be published to enormous critical acclaim ('A magnificent biography'. 'A wonderful achievement'. 'A great biography, and a great work of art'. 'Tina Courtland's Life of Joseph Brandon is one of the major publishing events of the last ten years; perhaps the major publishing event since Miss Courtland's last book appeared. Cool, brilliantly written, and entirely honest, it tells us, as all great biographies do, and all biographies should, not only of one man's life, but of the lives of all of us'.), and be tipped to receive prizes as best biography of the year on both sides of the Atlantic.

And in the last three months of those two years she allowed herself to be bullied by Maisie into going to London and New York to give interviews and make television appearances (and allowed herself furthermore, in spite of a constant longing to be back in her home in Italy, to have a good time); she wondered continually (especially after she did return home) when she would hear from Margaret Brandon; and she was made very nervous by an amused telephone call from Christopher, who told her he had, as it happened, met Margaret at a party a few days before, and had been asked by her for Tina Courtland's address.

'I am going to Italy for a holiday,' the woman had said. 'I would like to pay her a visit.'

'What was she like?' Tina asked.

'Like? The same as ever, of course. Only more so possibly. There used to be an occasional expression on her face. Now there's no trace of one, ever.'

'Did she mention the book?'

'Not really. She just murmured that she was glad you'd had such a great success with it.'

'Oh,' Tina said; and then 'Did she tell you exactly when she'd be coming?'

'To you?' Christopher laughed. 'No. But she's leaving for Italy tomorrow. I expect she'll get in touch.'

Margaret Brandon didn't get in touch, however; she simply drove up unannounced one afternoon, in a hired car.

Tina, who had thought that she might do just that, was, as ever, working in the garden when she heard the car coming up the long stony road to the house; and guessed immediately who the visitor was. And though she had been so nervous when

27

she had received Christopher's call, as she brushed her hands on her trousers and went up to greet the woman, she realized that now the meeting itself was upon her, she no longer was.

In fact, she realized, she was only curious; and glad that this last scene was about to be played.

Physically Margaret Brandon hadn't changed at all; unless, as Christopher had said, she seemed even more perfectly embalmed than she had been two years ago. Yet as Tina accompanied her into the house, she had the feeling that there was a purpose about that slim, beautifully dressed body that she didn't remember from their previous meeting. Then the woman had been like an exquisite objet d'art; a hard polished thing drained of all life, and useless except for the relaxation it might, to admirers of such objects, give to the eye. Now, while she *was* more brilliant, more finished, more, in her way, perfect than ever, she had an air of having found some sense in her very hardness. It was as if a diamond, that had always been worn in a ring, had, after a final polish, suddenly become aware that it could, if it wished to, cut.

The explanation for this unexpected air of purpose was, Tina had no doubt, that she had come here to say something; something about the book.

She started, however, as she accepted a glass of wine, by murmuring—for the third time since she had arrived—that she was so sorry just to drop in like this, but she had been passing and had been given the address by Christopher. She went on to assure Tina she wouldn't keep her from her work in the garden for very long—she was on her way to visit her sister-in-law, who was staying about thirty miles away—and to tell her how beautiful she found the house, how tranquil it was up here, and how she envied her. And she concluded her warm-up, so to speak, by recounting everything she had done since she had arrived in Italy.

But then, as she took a seat, lowered her eyes, and paused

before delivering whatever speech she had prepared, something strange happened. Which was that Tina, who had been nervous while waiting for the woman, and merely curious for the last few minutes, now all at once became terrified, and realized she didn't want to hear that speech. For just as she had been certain, before she had read them, of what Brandon's diaries would reveal, now she was certain of what Brandon's widow was going to say. She was going to say—Tina *knew*—that she had trusted Tina, as a woman and as a writer, and that Tina had betrayed her. That even if she hadn't been aware of it at the time, or felt capable of taking the responsibility, she had, ultimately, handed over her husband's diaries in the hope that Tina would have the strength and courage to disclose their contents to the world. And finally, that being now so very desperate, so very aware that this was her last chance—or finding, simply, that with Brandon two years dead *she* now had the courage, and could take the responsibility—she had decided to publish the diaries (of which she had presumably made photocopies) herself; and so be free of the lies and deceptions in which her marriage had involved her. The lies and deceptions that had been bred by her refusal to acknowledge what she had always suspected or perhaps always, within her, known. The lies and deceptions that had caused her to become the frozen, stone-like creature that she was today. . . .

And if that were to happen, Tina thought, not only would that foulness be released into the world, but she herself would, more than ever, be caught up in the ensuing scandal.

So terrified was she by this prospect, and by her conviction that this was the speech Margaret Brandon was preparing to make, that even as the woman murmured 'I read your book about Joe,' she interrupted her with a forced laugh, said 'Oh before we talk about that I'd like you to meet my friend,' and, not caring how extraordinary her behaviour must appear, rushed to the door and shouted for Maisie—who was upstairs writing an article for some medical journal—to come down. And though as she hovered in the hallway she thought that perhaps she had made matters worse—for if Margaret Brandon made her speech in front of Maisie it would be not only appalling, but humiliating—she also thought that she didn't care. She just had to put it off for as long as possible; and she couldn't be alone if it weren't possible to put it off altogether.

But when she returned into the living room with Maisie, something stranger still than her being overcome with terror happened; something truly amazing. As Margaret Brandon looked at her—and showed she had noted that terror—an expression came into her eyes. . . .

For a moment Tina was too confused to know what she was saying, as she introduced Maisie. She must have been mistaken, she told herself. There couldn't have been an expression—not in *those* eyes. It was impossible. Absolutely impossible. And certainly not such an expression as the one she had seen. An expression of pity, and understanding, and the most terrible resignation.

But there had been; and she was to see it again, just ten minutes later. She was to see it as she and Maisie walked Margaret Brandon to her car, as Margaret Brandon thanked them for their hospitality and told them yet again how much she envied them their home, and as Margaret Brandon returned once more, as Tina knew at last she must, to the subject of the book.

She returned to the subject of the book; but she didn't say what she had come to say, and had been on the point of saying earlier. No—all she said now, with pity, understanding, and the most terrible resignation not only in her eyes, but in her voice too, was this: that she had thought the biography very well written, that she expected Tina must be very proud of it

—and that she had wanted to come here in person 'To thank you, Tina, for telling the truth.'

Then, for a moment, Tina felt more than confused. She felt —along with an immense sense of gratitude, and an even more immense sense of awe at the sacrifice that was being made on her behalf—a chill come over her. A chill that threatened to make her—as the news of Brandon's death, two years ago, had threatened to make her—faint. It was the same chill that had frozen the woman in front of her; and it was a chill that was caused by the idea that in those words the whole of Joseph Brandon's horror had, after all, been revealed to her.

No, she wanted to scream. Not that. Please not that. *That* I cannot bear.

But bear it she did; as, she realized a minute later, after Margaret Brandon had climbed into her car, given a last tired smile—a smile of total defeat—and started the motor, she would be able to bear even her return to the world. A return made inevitable, as she had feared it would be, and saw now was, by that revelation of horror. In fact, she thought, giving a wave of farewell to her visitor, with the example of that wonderful woman before her, there would be nothing henceforth she couldn't bear.

The Travelling Companion

HE WAS TEMPTED, since it came from abroad, not to open it. Precisely because it came from abroad, he did open it.

And therein, he was to think later, lay the seeds of the whole affair.

Andrew Stairs was a big bouncing boy of a man—forty-five years and three months old the day the letter arrived—with a smooth red cherubic face and the manner of a clumsy good-natured puppy, and he distrusted all things foreign as much as he was fascinated by them. The distrust was due to his loving his own country to such an extent that whatever was not British he considered corrupt, barbarous or at any rate in some way inferior; the fascination to the fact that—however unwilling he might be to admit it—even he was aware, and acknowledged, that though Britain was an island, islands were hardly more isolated from the rest of the world than any other place, that what went on, for better or worse (normally for worse) in the rest of the world had an effect on the life of islands, and above all, that corruption and barbarity had an attraction—for him—that integrity and civilization simply couldn't match. Of course he didn't imagine that Britain was without corruption or barbarity, and when he heard or came across instances of either he was both ashamed and distressed. Yet he couldn't help feeling that such lapses were lapses from the norm; vile blemishes on an otherwise perfect portrait. Whereas abroad—the lapse was the norm; the portrait itself was vile. And therefore, having more practice, in this field at least foreigners were better; their sins were altogether more vivid, more brightly-coloured, more—unfortunately—splendid.

This mixture of distrust and fascination coloured not only the way he thought; it had also given shape to his career. (And thereby had become, to a large degree, the central feature of his existence.)

He was a writer. He was successful. He was happy to be both a writer and successful, and his stories were always, essentially, the same. (Partly because having found a recipe that was popular he saw no reason to change the dish he served; and partly because however many times he did serve it, and regardless of the fact that it was popular, he still liked it himself.) They were always set in the English countryside, were always peopled by characters who were products of that countryside—who had, after generations, come to resemble the fields and hills that surrounded them, the trees that protected them, the winds that blew upon them—and always, in one way or another, described how these characters were affected—invariably disastrously—by the arrival in their midst of a foreigner. (Only once had there been a 'happy ending', but it hadn't really been convincing, and the book had been the least successful, in critical and popular opinion alike, of all his works.) They were, in short, gentle rustic tragedies; and they pretended to be nothing more.

Yet though he was happy with his career, and with his life as a writer, he wasn't entirely satisfied by either. Two things in particular troubled him.

The first—and less serious—source of dissatisfaction was the fact that his books were sometimes accused of encouraging racial prejudice; or prejudice of all kinds. It was a charge he refuted utterly—he believed he helped to explain the causes of prejudice; a necessary pre-requisite if it were to be stamped out—but it did, nevertheless, hurt.

The second thing that troubled him was, however, a graver

concern; and it was that he had never, not even for a day trip to Calais, been abroad. And while he longed to—to see the vile portrait first hand, to experience the sensation of being a foreigner himself, and to push back the boundaries of his consciousness (and thereby give his work a greater scope?)—he was afraid. He didn't, ridiculous though he knew it was, dare to leave his beloved island. Not, at any rate, alone. And so far he had never met anyone with whom he could have travelled who would have been both protective, but would also have stood aside and allowed him to feel the full heat of the flames upon his face. What he wanted was a Virgil who would lead him through Hell—but a Virgil who would only hold his hand, and not try to stand between the fires of Hell and the vision of Andrew Stairs. Someone, in other words, who would not interpret, explain, or otherwise attempt to be a medium.

His wife, in the fifteen years of their marriage, had often volunteered to be such a guide, and tried to convince him that she could give him both support and freedom. But he had always had to refuse. For so similar were they in outlook he wouldn't have been able to help seeing things through her eyes most of the time. Furthermore, though she went abroad herself occasionally and always returned unscathed, he didn't want her to be exposed to any danger; as, he was sure, she would have been exposed if she had gone with him. Because once in a while she might have seen things through *his* eyes; and seen, in spite of her previous travels, what she had never seen before. Seen, that is, too much.

His being so troubled, his longing so much to go abroad, and his searching, if only in the back of his mind, for some ideal travelling companion, were probably the reasons why, having opened that letter with its foreign—US—stamp, and having read it two or three times, he did something he had seldom done before to a 'fan' letter coming, as they sometimes came, from overseas. Which was reply to it.

34

Though possibly it wasn't for any of the above reasons that he took this unusual step, but just because it arrived on a bright sunny morning which happened to be the fourth of May; which also happened to be the second anniversary of Jill's death. (She had been killed in a road accident; in a head-on collision with another car; driven, ironically, by another writer. A man whom Andrew detested. An American. . . .) And thinking of her—and being charmed by the tone of his unknown correspondent; who was, he gathered, a twenty-three-year-old girl who had just graduated from Berkeley—he realized how very much he still missed his wife, how lonely he was, and how he should try, now, to put aside his mourning and form some new relationship.

Not that he imagined for a moment—even if his motives for replying were that he was lonely, and that to continue mourning Jill was not only fruitless but wrong—that Lucinda Grey, as the Californian girl signed herself, would be the person with whom he would form a relationship. The idea of marrying or having any sort of rapport with a foreigner was inconceivable to him. How could creatures who were nurtured in different soils, and shaped by different winds, ever really have anything in common apart, perhaps, from a mutual dislike of their native soils and winds? They couldn't; and dislike of one's own land, of one's own self (for to him the person *was* the country) was not a satisfactory basis for a relationship. One might just as well expect a cat to mate with a dog. Oh certainly they were both animals, both needed food and drink, both needed shelter and protection from the elements. But apart from that there was, frankly, nothing. (He would admit that there were exceptions to this general rule; but very few. Far fewer than most people would have claimed.)

I am merely, he told himself, as he wrote his own letter, being polite. Responding to kindness with kindness. And accepting the notion that I must start being more sociable, meeting new people, putting out, however tentatively, feelers.

He could tell himself what he liked; and did. Nevertheless, rendered defenceless by his very inability to imagine that Lucinda Grey could ever be anything other than unknown, and by his very conviction that feelers should be extended only in one's own country, by September of that year the unthinkable had happened. Andrew Stairs had fallen in love.

It was, he thought, as he stood in the small flat he had taken as a pied-à-terre in London (taken, two months before, ostensibly as part of his campaign to be more sociable, but actually because he had started to realize, alone in his cottage in Sussex, the danger he was in; and had thought London might save him from it) more than unthinkable. It was insane. He *couldn't* be in love. Not with someone he had never met. Not with someone who hadn't been born and bred in England. He couldn't be.

But he was.

He wasn't sure, even now, what had caused the collapse.

That first letter *had* been charming, and inriguing; there had been a lightness about it, a lack of earnestness, and a pleasant touch of irony that would have been remarkable coming from a fifty-year-old. Coming as it did from a twenty-three-year-old, it was so remarkable that it bordered on—but did not cross the border of—archness. However, it had been nothing more than remarkable, and in the past he had, once or twice, received other remarkable letters; to which he had also replied. But that had been the end of the matter; and he hadn't come even to like his correspondents, let alone to love them.

He supposed the trouble had started with the second letter; that had been written and sent before his reply to the first had been received. Because whereas the first, while telling him very little of the writer, had been filled mainly with gentle, generally complimentary remarks about his books—together with one or two less complimentary remarks on his apparent racism—the second had hardly mentioned his work, and had been filled with casual chatter about the character and the day to day life of Lucinda Grey; as if Andrew Stairs were an old friend, and would be interested in such things. The wonder was—he was. He couldn't help himself. Once more it was probably the tone of the piece more than the actual words which caught him. But he found himself fascinated by Lucinda's passing comments on some new film she had seen, on the number of times she washed her hair, on the temporary work she was doing in a hospital while trying to decide what to do with her recently received degree in modern languages; and rivetted by the story of her family. Her mother, she said, had been a poor, sad, alcoholic little woman of Scottish descent, who had worked all her life as a waitress, and who had once—her brief moment of glory?—had an affair, or anyway gone to bed with, a wealthy, childless businessman. A baby—Lucinda herself—had been born as a result of this affair, and the businessman had set up a trust fund for the education of his daughter. Shortly after he had done so, he had had a stroke, and died; leaving the remainder of his money to some distant cousin. The result was that Lucinda had been educated at some of the most expensive if not the best schools in the States, had been, nevertheless, penniless throughout her youth, and had been given a rare insight into the worlds of the almost entirely dispossessed, and of the almost entirely possessing.

Andrew didn't necessarily believe this tale—it sounded to him a little too much like a fantasy; though whether of a rich girl or a poor girl he wasn't certain—but he was enthralled nevertheless; and moved to write again himself. If only, he told himself, to comment on the parallels that Lucinda chose to see between his books and her own life. 'I used to feel,' she wrote, 'that I was one of your "foreigners"; only doubly so. I was a foreigner in the moneyed world of my school-fellows, and came to hate their arrogance, their smugness, and above all their, in general, strange lack of vitality (as if they lived both figuratively and literally off the blood of others, were therefore both more dependent on others and more frightened of others than those others were on them and of them, and thought their best defence against such dependence and fear was an almost total retreat into passivity and the most rigid conformity); and I was a foreigner in the poor and mostly uneducated world of my mother and her few friends, and came to hate their submissiveness, their, deep-down, *approval* of the way things were and of their own misery, and above all their lack of rage. (If not against the world, at least against themselves.) What was more, what *is* more, again like one of your foreigners, whenever anyone "loved" me—my mother, two (so far) men—or even became friendly with me, I tended to confuse them, and bring disasters on them. (My mother virtually killed herself with drink; towards the end—she died five years ago—I'm convinced she realized why I used to get mad at her, wanted, or maybe tried to feel the rage I wished she would feel, but by then no longer had the strength; and the two men both destroyed themselves within a year of our meeting. One became a heroin addict; the other burned himself alive. They were both, before the relationship started, on the surface at least self-confident, intelligent boys of "good" families. My fault? No, theirs obviously; a part of them was already searching for foreignness. They found it in me; but they couldn't cope with it when they did find it.)

'Maybe I'm romanticising, trying to make myself more interesting than I am. If that is the case you can put it down to youth, or inexperience, or—whatever you like!'

A passage from the third letter read: 'You said you have never been abroad, want to, but are frightened. Maybe you should come to the States. I'll be your guide!'

From the fourth letter: 'I'm tall and blond, since you ask;

but I'm not going to send you a photograph. You can imagine me as you please, if you please.'

From the fifth: 'I've never felt that foreign countries are corrupt and barbarous. Though to be honest, in strictly political terms, in 96 per cent of cases I guess I do. Even your old island, with its monarchy, the empty, pompous (somehow *lying*) voices of your politicians and so-called upper classes, and the grey dispiriting lack of *joy* I've found in most Englishmen and women I've met, strikes me, who's never been there!, as being in, and being, a pretty sorry state. (Notwithstanding the fact that we're no slouches here when it comes to corruption and barbarity.) What I have felt, however, is that foreign countries are like different, so far unexplored, and possibly inaccessible areas of my self. My conscious self—my conscious reality, let's say—is American. But behind that there are whole other continents, climates, mountains, deserts—whole other realities—that affect my conscious self, have gone to make up my conscious self (as if America were merely a crust that had formed on the surface of a pool), and are all part of my total being.

'What I have also felt—and feel today more strongly than ever—is a great desire to visit, in my lifetime, as many of those other continents and climates as I can. Oh God, Andrew, you must think I am crazy—but I want to travel, travel, travel!'

To this Andrew replied: 'No, I don't think you are crazy, but I do think you are wrong. I'll agree that England is my conscious reality, as America is yours. But beyond that I won't go. For I believe that outside of England everything is a dream; or must be considered, for the sake of order and sanity, a dream. (Just as a Frenchman must consider everything outside France a dream; and an Italian etc, etc.) One *has* to live in one's own reality, and not be tempted by dreams. Or to use your image, one has to stay in the crust that has formed one, and which one helps to form. Because pools (and concepts

39

such as "total beings") are too vast, too deep; they are disturbed by treacherous currents; and one can drown in them.

'Having said which—of course I *am* tempted by dreams, I *should* like to swim—and maybe, one day, I will take you up on your offer of showing me round the States.'

It was soon after he had written this that Andrew became aware of the danger he was in; and abruptly leaving the cottage where he had lived uninterruptedly for the last seventeen years, took the furnished flat in London.

Lucinda, in her next letter, wrote: 'Seriously, why don't you come?' She also wrote, 'Do you realize we have a rather strange relationship? I feel I know you better than anyone I have ever met in my life.'

A month later: 'I know this sounds stupid, but—I think I am in love with you.'

For three weeks Andrew didn't reply. Then, on the morning of 23 September, he could contain himself no longer; and in a state of excitement sent a telegram which read: 'I think I am with you too.'

But it wasn't till that afternoon, as he stood in his flat in Queensgate, looking out of the window at the pale autumnal sky, that he told himself—having calmed down now—that what he had said in his telegram was true. . . .

He spent the next month attempting to find some solution to his problem. That there was a solution he didn't doubt. There had to be. He might be in love with this mysterious Californian; she might be in love with him. But nothing could come of such a love. For if it did, it would involve one or other of them leaving their own country, and settling abroad. Which was out of the question for him; and which he could neither approve of for her, nor wish upon anyone he loved. So—

At the end of October he wrote: 'You realize our correspondence must come to an end; that the situation is impossible.'

Lucinda's reply was: 'Don't be ridiculous. There's no reason for our *correspondence* to end. I don't see why we can't have an affair by mail.'

'Because sooner or later we shall be tempted to meet—or rather will succumb to the temptation to meet.'

'Well? It might be a good thing. We might hate each other if we actually met. And if you really are afraid of coming here, I can always come to England.'

'You can't. Because then you would be a foreigner.'

'I was only proposing to *visit* you. Not move in, sight un- seen. However, if everything were okay when we met, and if you really couldn't face the idea of living with a foreigner (*I* wouldn't mind living anywhere if I loved someone, I think), we could spend six months here, six months there. That way we would both be at home for half the year, and the other half would have to be the price to be paid for—well, happiness, or whatever you like to call it.'

'I think it would be too high a price. It would ruin both of us.'

'Oh Andrew—do you really think we are so very awful here?'

'No, of course I don't. But as I think I've said before, aside from the moral (and therefore, ultimately, physical?) danger of living abroad, of trying to live with, through one's "total being" (sorry to keep throwing that phrase in your face; but by total being what I think you mean is the whole world, and the whole world *is* too big, at least for me; I can only cope with that little segment of it that is called England), I have always considered that one's own country is like one's own body. (*Is* one's own body.) And if this is so, one must not only respect all parts of that body, and try to prevent any one part of it from dictating to, controlling, or abusing the other parts (for if you don't those other parts will become infected and diseased, and will eventually destroy you), but one must also, I believe (though Christians may not approve, and I may sound unfortunately like some self-help manual), if one is ever to care for something and someone else—or even live in peace with something or someone else—first care for, and live in peace with, one's own body. What you are proposing is that we should both desert our own bodies for six months of the year. Which is treason. I can understand how people wish to desert their own bodies for a couple of weeks a year. But for six months? No, no, and no again! In more practical terms, I couldn't bear to miss a spring here. Or a summer or an autumn. Or a winter. To see how the trees change colour, the birds migrate, the flowers bud, bloom, fade, die—and then bud again. To see how people change from day to day, how their expressions, their moods, their clothes alter with the weather, to see how they cope with crises, with national disasters, or national triumphs—with personal tragedies and personal joys. And above all I couldn't bear to think that I wasn't attempting, every single day of my life, and in my tiny, insignificant way— either by writing something, talking to a friend, merely giving someone a direction in the street—to make myself, though it may sound revoltingly priggish, *better*. And by making myself better, making my country better. Improving, if you like, if but minutely, the reality in which I live. There! I've never said so much to anyone, and I blush to so expose myself. But that is, essentially, what I believe, what I work for, what I want. And I could not, or cannot, consider renouncing any of it. It would, again, not be *like* renouncing my life—it *would* be renouncing my life.'

Crossly, Lucinda fired back: 'In one of your books you say "I distrust people who claim to be citizens of the world, and to love all mankind. They tend to be people who are at home nowhere, not even with themselves, and to like no one in particular—least of all themselves." And I'm with you there. But you go to the opposite extreme. Caring for yourself first might be healthy and good; to care *only* for yourself strikes me as being as unhealthy and bad as hating yourself. For by your own token, if you do care for your own little part of the world to the exclusion of all else—those other parts might well become infected and diseased, and destroy you.

'One last point. By writing you say you want to improve yourself/your country. But why *not* widen your scope, and take on the whole world? For aside from the fact that it *isn't* too big, and that—if you'll excuse the misquote—"no island is an island", you wouldn't at all be renouncing life; you would be living more intensely, more fully. And your books would be correspondingly more intense, more full.'

To this Andrew could give but one reply; and he gave it, in a single sheet of paper. 'You may well be right. But I am afraid, I am afraid—and the answer must still be no.'

And there, for the next few months, the matter rested. No further word passed between the English writer and the American girl. What Lucinda did with herself Andrew had no idea; what he did was spend two or three days a week in London, meeting as many new people as he could, and the rest of the time in his cottage. He worked. He read. He listened to music. He had friends come to stay with him; he went to stay with friends. Yet through all this period, and though he did get to know several new people whom he liked—becoming particularly fond of an austere reserved woman who was a Labour councillor in Manchester—he could not forget his unknown mistress, as he had come to think of her. In fact, as the weeks went by, from being in love with her he became obsessed with her. He imagined that she was the most beautiful—in every sense of the word—girl in the world. He imagined that she would be the guide to Hell he had been searching for; the one person who would both allow him to see all the sights, and keep him safe. He imagined that she would be the exception to his rule; that she would be the one person who could live in a foreign country, and be loved, without bringing destruction upon her lover. He imagined even that with her by his side he *would* be able to take on the entire world, *would* be able to cope with it; and would, as a result, and as she had suggested, be able to write a book that really summed the whole thing up; that would, possibly, be an infinitesimally small step in improving the whole sorry business; and would, in any case, be better than anything he had done so far. He thought of her by day, when he worked; he thought of her at night, as he lay in bed. And the more he thought of her the more wonderful she became in his imagination, until she had almost ceased to be a real human being at all. She had become a vision, an ideal, a goddess. She no longer, in his mind, ate, or slept, laughed or talked; she simply hovered above him leading him on, blinding him with her light.

He fought against such nonsense, telling himself that she was just a perfectly ordinary girl who probably had bad breath, a moral squint, and an emotional hunch-back, to whom he would hardly be able to talk if they did meet, and with whom he had nothing at all in common; and telling his friends about his postal affair as it were just a huge joke. But while, when he did tell himself these things, and laughed with his friends, he succeeded in demolishing the image of Lucinda Grey for five minutes, after those five minutes had passed he realized his obsession had grown still greater. He re-read her letters constantly, trying to convince himself that there was nothing special about them, that they didn't suggest anything special about their writer, and that they were no more than the reasonably intelligent outpourings of some literary groupie, and he looked repeatedly at photographs of Jill, reminding himself that theirs had been a real love—that of two adults who could give themselves to each other without fear that their gift would be mishandled or abused—and repeating to himself that he had only become involved with Lucinda because he was lonely, and loneliness was not to be confused with love.

But it was all no use. . . . Finally, at the end of March, he could fight no longer. All right, he told himself, he was mad. All right, he was likely to be disillusioned. All right, he was playing with fire. Nevertheless, he *was* in love; and he was going to do something about it. Something practical, such as—

He was never to know what—if he hadn't, the day after making this resolution, received a phone call from an old friend—he would have done. Though he suspected, even then, it would have been nothing. Because he still didn't want to go to the States himself, he didn't want Lucinda to come to England in case she should prove less than ideal, and he could see no other alternative. But he *did*, one late March evening, receive a phone call from an old friend; and that changed everything.

The name of this friend was Fraser; and he was not only an old friend, and a good friend (his oldest, and best; though they didn't see each other very often, and hadn't been in touch at all for over nine months) but was also a person who played a particular part in the life of Andrew Stairs.

He was a tall, dark, impeccably dressed man with the sort of clipped British voice that many foreigners thought was the typical British voice, but which many Englishmen—or anyway Andrew, and most of their mutual friends—realized was the voice of an unhappy, at times nearly unbalanced man (it was too clipped; and almost imperceptibly hesitant); and just as Andrew 'Stayed in England' so Fraser 'Travelled'.

'Looking for love,' he would invariably say, when asked why he spent most of his adult life travelling through jungles, icy wastes, or the slums of big and foreign cities; and also invariably add, with an ironic laugh, 'donchyeknow.' But there again, while the laugh and the expression might have fooled most foreigners and some Englishmen, it did not fool Fraser's friends; who knew that what he had said was the literal truth. The antithesis of Andrew, he searched the earth looking for the ideal companion with whom he could go, and stay forever, home. So far—aged forty-four, with three marriages, innumerable affairs, and five books about his travels behind him—he hadn't found his ideal; and was more and more prepared to admit it was likely he never would. But he hadn't yet abandoned hope; and knew that until he did—which would come either with his death, or be the cause of his death—he was bound, or doomed, to go on searching.

The particularity of his friendship with Andrew was due not to their diametrically opposed life-styles (that indeed was the explanation of why they were friendly at all; each admired, and envied—though also, if without rancour, pitied and despised—the other's chosen way), nor even to his sincere profession that Andrew's books were among the few modern works he unreservedly liked (a profession that Andrew, with equal sincerity, made with regard to Fraser's books). No, what made it so special was this: Fraser provided Andrew with background material for his novels. If the stay at home novelist had, as his outsider, a literal foreigner (which he did in half his books), and if, for example, he decided that this character were to be Indian, then he would wait till Fraser was in England, invite him to the cottage for a few days, and spend hours—sometimes as many as seven at a stretch—listening as that clipped desperate voice described not just in great detail, but in memorable, and evocative detail, the light, the atmosphere, the smell of the city, or even the village, from which the fictional man or woman came. He would tell Andrew what it was like to buy stamps in a post-office; what the noise-scape of the chosen place was like; what the precise colour of the sky was at dawn. And the—to Andrew—miraculous thing was (which was part of the reason why he admired the man's books), so totally could Fraser lose himself in these details, so entirely could he *become* the thing he was describing, that he not only saw, heard, smelled all the things he told of from an Indian point of view—there was no suggestion of the English observer abroad—but also told of them as no Indian that Andrew had ever met had been able to. Possibly because those Indians had been too familiar with their native sights and sounds to be completely aware of them; or possibly because Fraser knew himself better—in Andrew's opinion—than anyone else in the world. In India, that is, he knew himself as an Indian. Just as in Mongolia, he knew himself as a Mongolian. There was, in fact, only one part of himself that Fraser did not know; only one country he could not describe. That country was England; and it was his lack of insight with regard to England alone that made his self-knowledge less than total. (And explained also, to Andrew's way of thinking, the desperation in his voice.)

The phone call that Fraser made that evening towards the end of March was, therefore, the phone call not only of a friend, but also of an already established envoy; of a minister, so to speak, of foreign affairs; and it changed everything because after the man had mentioned that he was going to be in England for a month, and after he had asked if he might come and stay in the country for a long weekend, he said that his next trip was to be Alaska and the Aleutian Islands—but that he was going via San Francisco. . . .

And the second he heard this Andrew knew he had found the solution to his problem.

'Would you,' he said, without the slightest hesitation, 'do me a favour when you're in San Francisco?'

'Course I would,' came the reply—as nearly without hesitation as Fraser could manage. 'What is it?'

'Well you see,' Andrew said; and went on to tell his fellow writer about the affair he had been having by post, and to ask him if he would mind calling Lucinda, meeting her, and then sending the most complete report possible about the girl. 'You can give her,' he added, 'the most complete report possible about me, too.'

47

'I shall do both, willingly,' Fraser said; and then changed the subject by asking Andrew when it would be convenient for him to come to the cottage. 'Shan't be alone, of course,' he clipped. 'Chinese girl.'

'You're sure you don't mind?' Andrew—who didn't want the subject changed just yet—insisted.

'Mind? Course I don't. Be delighted to. Glad you asked me.'

'I'm,' Andrew said, 'glad you're going.'

And so he was—for he could think of no one whose report he would sooner have had, or whose report he would sooner have trusted—and so he remained for the next few days. He was more than glad; he was overjoyed, and came to think of Fraser's intervention as little short of divine. But after those few days had passed, and the weekend of Fraser's visit approached, doubts entered his mind; and his joy became shadowed by fear.

The doubts and fears were not occasioned by any sudden lack of faith in Fraser's report on Lucinda; that he knew would be honest, and absolutely reliable. They were rather occasioned by a sudden lack of faith in Fraser himself—and even a certain lack of faith in Lucinda. The latter he was, after he had thought about it for a while, almost able to dismiss—after all, how could he, or why should he, have faith in someone he didn't know—but the lack of faith in Fraser was a more serious concern; and one that grew more profound the more he thought about it.

What if, Andrew couldn't help asking himself, Lucinda *is* the rare creature I imagine her to be? What if she is a person of true beauty; a person of total integrity? Of course it was extremely unlikely; total integrity in this world was, for all practical purposes, impossible; and anyone possessing it would be more than rare; they would indeed be ideal. But just suppose for a moment—she *were*? Mightn't Fraser, who was searching the world for such a person, fall in love with her

48

himself? Or better, mustn't Fraser, given his character, fall in love with her himself? Yes, Andrew answered himself miserably; he must. And maybe Lucinda, when she met him. . . .

People who knew Fraser only slightly, or not at all—those who thought him typically British, and were fooled by his irony—claimed to find the effect he had on women incomprehensible. 'How could anyone,' Andrew had often been asked, 'fall in love with such an absurdity? He's a throwback; he's a caricature; he is the most negative, sexless man on the face of this earth.' But Andrew, who had more than once seen Fraser's first meeting with a woman he had subsequently become involved with, believed he understood perfectly. For one thing, when Fraser was attracted to someone he immediately, if without being conscious of it, revealed that his British veneer was but the thinnest of disguises, and wasn't at all to be taken seriously; for another he gave the impression—the correct impression—that just as he could immerse himself in and become a foreign country, so he could, and was more than willing to, immerse himself in and become a 'foreign' person (which complete abdication was unnerving; if only because it denoted a courage that was appalling); and for yet another he gave the (again correct?) impression that beneath his thin disguise there was not really a person at all, but simply a void; a black hole of terrifying proportions.

Once Andrew had tried to explain the matter to some wondering woman. 'You see,' he said, 'if Fraser didn't give himself away, he would be sucked down and disappear into his own darkness. By becoming someone else he manages to save himself—at least for as long as the affair lasts. Unfortunately none of the women who have accepted him completely have ever managed to save themselves.'

Some—and how terrifyingly similar, Andrew reflected now, their fates sounded to those of Lucinda's two lovers—had taken to drink; some had joined strange cults. Several, he knew, had

49

had total breakdowns; several more had killed themselves. . . .

'Only then, when they have been destroyed, when a sacrifice, if you like, has been made to the pit, does Fraser re-emerge; and start to look again for the woman who will be able to accept him, yet have the strength not to fall into the darkness. Or better perhaps, for the woman who will make him accept himself; and by doing so, give *him* the strength to resist that fall.'

As he had tried to uproot the obsession that Lucinda had become, so now Andrew tried to uproot his doubts and fears regarding Fraser. But just as he had failed with the one, so he failed with the other; and by the Friday when Fraser was due to arrive at the cottage, doubts and fears had turned to panic; and a near certainty that what he had foreseen would happen.

The most ridiculous, yet disturbing aspect of the matter was that while now he had come to the conclusion that Fraser was the last person on earth he should send on this mission, he was still certain—more than ever certain—that Fraser was the only person on earth he could send. Because the man was going to San Francisco anyway, which seemed as if destiny had singled him out for the task. Because Fraser *was* his oldest and closest friend (it had been Fraser who had introduced him to Jill; Fraser the person he had called when Jill had been killed), and in such circumstances one could only rely on the oldest and closest of friends. And because there was the indisputable fact that if Lucinda were the ideal creature for whom he had been searching, Fraser alone would be sure to recognize her.

Yet though he knew he could ask no one else, as Andrew bumped, blushed and blundered through the weekend—he was continually dropping things, knocking things over, saying things he didn't mean to say, and generally giving even more of an impression of a red and gauche (if good-natured) schoolboy than he normally did—his panic grew to such an extent that he was more than once tempted to tell Fraser that everything was off, that he had changed his mind, that Lucinda had gone away, that—that Fraser wasn't to go to see her. (Apart from anything else, he couldn't help thinking, surely Lucinda, if she had a grain of sense, would prefer the dark demonic travel writer, with his core of blackness, to a clumsy, maladroit forty-five-year-old adolescent. . . .)

Fraser realized that Andrew was disturbed about something, and he might have guessed about what (for having remarked, with a smile, the evening of his arrival, 'I hope I don't find your beloved Californian too attractive'—and having noted the manic laughter with which his words were greeted—he was very careful thereafter to mention Lucinda, and his forthcoming examination of her, only with the greatest seriousness); but since the novelist didn't mention his fears to him, he pretended to take the blushes and clumsiness as signs only of love. 'I never believed I would see the day,' he said gravely, 'that Andrew Stairs sighed for a foreigner.'

If *only*, Andrew thought, he had the courage to go to America himself. But he didn't; and if he had managed to force himself into going, he would have been so nervous— nervous of the country, nervous of the continent, nervous of just being abroad, alone—that even if Lucinda had been more wonderful that he dreamed he wouldn't have been able to see that wonder, and would have lost her forever. No—he *couldn't* go abroad until after he had found his travelling companion; and the only way to find her was to put his trust in Fraser.

But—Oh God, he thought for the hundredth time. Oh God. Just suppose. . . .

His panic reached a climax on the Monday morning, as his guests were preparing to leave; when Fraser, taking him aside for a moment, asked him what he thought of the Chinese girl (whom Andrew, so distraught had he been, and so preoccupied with Fraser, had hardly been aware of), told him that he himself didn't think too much of her (she was sweet enough;

51

but she only hovered and never—wisely, Andrew felt—landed), and confessed that he was going through a particularly bad time at the moment. (He was more and more often tempted, he said, simply to curl up in a corner somewhere and fall asleep, forever. He also, at times, came near to hating Andrew, so much did he envy him his cottage, his peace, his *acceptance* of himself.) But after he had listened to this cry of despair, after he had tried, as best he could, to reassure Fraser that he would eventually find what he was looking for, and when he still, in spite of the near hysteria that that cry and its implications had induced in him, hadn't countermanded his orders regarding Lucinda, Andrew realized that the worst was over; and that from now on, though his fears would remain with him, he could only sit back, wait, and leave matters in the hands of the gods.

In fact he left them so very much in their hands over the following weeks that it wasn't till two days before Fraser's departure for the States, when the man called to say goodbye, that it occurred to Andrew he hadn't written to Lucinda to warn her of his friend's arrival. (That he hadn't written at all for months, nor heard from her—and that she might now have forgotten him, be in love with someone else, or have left Berkeley—didn't seem to him to be causes for concern. For aside from the fact that they hadn't broken with each other—and that, therefore, their mutual silence, long though it had been, couldn't be viewed as other than a pause in the dialogue, a moment for gathering breath before the great, the conclusive statement was made—the affair had assumed in his mind such mythic proportions that it would have been unworthy to admit the possibility of her doing anything so mundane as forget him, move house, or fall for some bearded, bespectacled philosophy graduate.) He debated with himself then whether to phone her, cable her, or send a note by special delivery. He was tempted to do the first, because he would have liked to have heard her voice. But eventually—after he'd realized that if he did phone he might be too tongue-tied to speak, and thought that a telegram would be too cryptic—he settled for the special delivery; hoping that it would arrive in time, and that Fraser wouldn't get in touch with her his very first day in San Francisco.

Having done it—and being at last so resigned he felt becalmed; a powerless ship waiting for the wind to arise—he placed himself once again in the hands of the gods; and, once again, waited.

He was not, however, to wait for very much longer. Only one more week.

The first letter was from Lucinda; a brief scrawl which read 'You might have warned me!' Whether the girl meant that she hadn't received his note, or that she should have been warned as to Fraser's character, Andrew wasn't certain.

The second letter, which arrived the day after, was also from Lucinda; and at least cleared up the above point. 'Have returned from mailing my protest to find your special delivery. So you did warn me. Anyway, your friend Fraser (first name? Last name? I asked him, but he wasn't forthcoming) called me yesterday afternoon, and in the evening we had dinner together. I guess you want a report on me! (Though we spent most of the time talking about you.) My first impression of him was that he was some sort of joke. My second that he was one of the strangest people I have ever met. By the time the evening ended—rather drunkenly on my part, and even more so on his, I suspect (though it's difficult to tell)—he had made me feel very uncomfortable indeed. I got home with the sensation—and it wasn't just the drink, I'm sure—that I had spent four hours peering down some really terrifyingly deep well. Or down the shaft of some mine whose ore is too dreadful to be extracted. And whereas I usually have a very good head for heights—for depths?—last night I suffered from vertigo.

He said he is going to be around for a few days more before moving north, and we both muttered something polite about getting together again. But while he may be an old friend of yours, and while he certainly is interesting, I sort of hope we don't. I mean I'm always grateful for a good meal, and I was curious to hear what he said about you. Only—I don't like to be uncomfortable, even less, I've discovered, do I like to suffer from vertigo, and I have the probably ridiculous feeling that to see too much of Mr Fraser is to lay oneself open to the risk of contamination. Though perhaps it isn't so ridiculous, because he said himself, during dinner, when we were talking about you, that you wear England about you like a lead shield, and that is one of the reasons why you can be friends. Which— at least now, in the sober (hungover) light of morning—seems a pretty odd thing to say, unless he does think of himself as emitting some kind of harmful rays. Anyway, if we do meet again, I shall go well protected; and shan't go too near the edge of that mine-shaft.

'One more thing. Fraser or no Fraser, I'm glad there is some link between us now, apart from our letters. I've often thought, over the past few months, that the forging of such a link was the next and necessary step if we were, eventually, to be—what? Joined . . . ? I would have attempted the task myself if I had known some ambassador I could trust to represent me. But unfortunately I didn't. Or don't. You, Andrew dear, are lucky.'

Andrew stared at this last sentence for a long time; then told himself that that remained to be seen.

As it still remained to be seen when Fraser's first letter arrived. For though the man gave no suggestion he might be seeing Lucinda again, and though (or just because) his first (and for Fraser generally sufficient) impression of the girl was everything that could have been wished for ('She is, super- ficially, good-humoured, unpretentious, intelligent, and aston- ishingly *conscious*; beneath the surface she struck me as being

not merely fine but truly—the only word for it—magnificent'),
Andrew couldn't help thinking that he wouldn't be entirely
happy, or entirely sure he *was* lucky to have an ambassador
such as Fraser, until he heard that the traveller had left San
Francisco, and gone north.

However, this reservation aside, he was—as he read and
re-read Fraser's letter, and realized that the next and necessary
step *now* (the final step, hopefully) was for him and Lucinda
to meet at last—almost entirely happy. It is, he thought, as he
read the letter again, too good to be true. . . .

He expected the news of Fraser's departure to be announced
in a second letter from the man; or in a third letter from
Lucinda. He also expected to receive this letter within two or
three days. When he didn't, he began to feel impatient. After
five days without news, he became worried. After a week he
became very worried. And after a fortnight he knew that what
he had feared *had* happened. It must have done. There could
be no other explanation now for the silence. Fraser and Lucinda
had indeed met again; and they had fallen in love. . . .

For a month then Andrew felt as miserable, as desperate,
as he had after Jill had been killed. Even more so perhaps. His
love for Jill had been a fact of the real world, of his day to
day existence; it had been a tangible thing that had been with
him for so long it had become a part of his body. When she
had died he had, after the initial shock, found comfort and
relief in the real world—in the company of friends, in the
company of music they had both liked, in the company of
books—and in the ritual of his daily life. He had felt her loss
as he would have felt the loss of part of his body; but the
body, as long as it is reasonably healthy, and the correct medi-
cations are applied, can recover from all but the most radical
of amputations. Whereas his love for Lucinda was not, to him,
a fact of the real world. It was an idealized love, such as he
might have dreamed of, or created in a story; it didn't—if only

55

because it hadn't had to, as yet—affect the course of his day to day existence. There was no worrying if Lucinda had a cold; no cause to celebrate if Lucinda had a birthday; no quiet continual sadness that had to be overcome about his and Lucinda's inability to conceive a child. And being so idealized, so out of this world, there was nothing, now that he had lost Lucinda, to comfort him. Nothing whatsoever remained of their relationship but a few letters; which in a couple of years would cease to mean anything. He had thought of their affair as being somehow mythic; he suffered now from a mythic hurt. He had longed, in the darker corners of his mind, to go abroad; he had found in Lucinda someone who could escort him there. Now, having lost her, he would never leave England. And though he loved it, and would always love it, he was afraid that having acknowledged his longing, brought it out into the open, and then had it frustrated, it would start to rot within him, go bad; and might, eventually, turn even his love for his own country into something sour, and disappointed, and joyless. What was more, having prepared as it were his foreign notebooks, been ready to write in them all that he observed abroad, and been eager to use those notes for some novel or novels that would be longer, deeper, more complete than any he had written so far, to have to put them away unused, and return to his former territory, might likewise eventually make that territory, which had hitherto pleased him, seem small, restricted, and unpleasant.

Losing Lucinda, he told himself, he had lost a chance of extending his life; and without her, the life that remained to him would become dull, and bitter. Weary, flat, stale and unprofitable. . . .

He spent that month alone in London, never answering his phone—though it rarely rang; few people knew he had taken the flat; fewer knew his number—only going out to visit galleries—to look at paintings which he found uninteresting—to visit theatres and cinemas—to see plays and films that he found tiresome—to walk through the spring-time parks—which should have delighted him, but in fact, feeling as he did cut off from all the growing life around him, depressed him, and struck him as being artificial and unnatural—and sometimes just to look at people, all of whose faces, including those of the young, seemed shaded by dullness, bitterness, and weariness.

At the end of the month, telling himself that he had to get off this train of misery he had boarded, and that it was nonsensical to stay in London—which he had never particularly liked, nor found particularly English—he returned to his cottage, hoping that his beloved countryside, and the familiar surroundings, would help to restore his spirits.

And for a day or two it seemed they would. The weather was wonderful—light and warm and clear—his garden—and the whole village—had rarely looked more green, more flower-filled, more peaceful and welcoming, and his neighbours, and the villagers in general, were so pleased to see him one would have thought he had been away for years, and that he were the favourite son of the entire community.

The old man who took care of his garden for him, and kept an eye on the cottage, said 'Don't seem right when you're away, Mr Stairs. Makes me feel like when they cut down all the elms.'

But after two days, and in spite of the warmth and the welcome—just walking round the village, after so short an absence, brought tears to his eyes, and made him conscious of how deeply rooted he was in this place, where he had lived for so long and which, even before he had lived there, he had always known (he had been born only seven miles away)—his sense of loss returned. And returned now—simply because, perhaps, he was so very much at home—with even greater force than before. He felt, though he had returned to the fold, that he had been excommunicated; or that he had been blown over by a terrible wind, so that though he was now back where he belonged, his roots, instead of being planted in the rich earth, and drawing nourishment from it, were facing up towards the sky, and were, before his eyes, withering.

He got angry with himself; telling himself that he was behaving like some adolescent who has just been jilted for the first time. He told himself he was being feeble, and weak, and self-pitying.

He tried to be philosophical; explaining to himself that of course he felt upset—a great love at forty-five, when there is less time left to enjoy it, is obviously more profound than a great love at twenty-five, when there is a whole lifetime ahead—and that what he was suffering from was not just a sentimental disappointment, but a crisis that many middle-aged people, especially when they are lonely, and are forced to accept that what they haven't done will never now be done, have to face; but that the pain would pass with time, and that as long as he propped himself up, and placed the earth firmly about him, his roots would once again take hold, and continue to feed him for many years. Indeed, having weathered the storm, he might very well grow even stronger than he had before, become even taller, more spreading, more firmly and irremovably a part of the land.

He tried thinking about his childhood and youth, and sought comfort in the memory of his parents. In the memory of his cobbler father, and of his mother who took in washing; those two kind people who had had him, their only child, so late in life, and had always encouraged him, from the moment he had started at the age of eight to make up stories, to be a writer. 'So you can tell,' he remembered his father saying, as they had walked over the Downs late one summer evening, and the old eyes had gazed across the hills as if they could see from one end of the country to another 'the truth.

If you tell the truth, people will recognize it. Even if they don't like it, they'll recognize it. And having recognized it they'll be more able to bear it. Or bear themselves. And that's all you can do in this world. Help other people, in one way or another, to bear it and themselves. Because if you don't you'll find that not only the world, but you yourself, are unbearable.'

He tried, even, to pour scorn upon the whole affair; telling himself that in a month or two he'd be ashamed of his own idiocy. A love-affair by post, indeed! It was grotesque.

But nothing he did, nothing he told himself, nothing he thought, helped him. He could not pick himself up, re-root himself; and he could not overcome his depression. And the very realization that this depression was such a vast and impregnable fortress made it become still more vast and impregnable. He felt that he were being pierced by arrows. That exposed on an open plain he were being rained on by stones. That boiling pitch were being poured over him, and shot were passing through his flesh. He started to hate his neat pretty village—it had become smug and self-satisfied—to hate the countryside around—its fertility became a cackle of derision over the sterility of the rest of the earth—and he started to hate his body. Great red, floppy, flabby thing; already dying, soon dead. . . .

He couldn't sleep at night; he couldn't work by day.

Oh Lucinda, he cried to the low-beamed ceiling of his bedroom, and to the small leaded window over his desk: Why did you ever write to me? Why did you say you loved me? And why did you ever encourage me to gaze into Hell; if you were not then going to accompany me there?

Oh why, he cried, oh why. . . .

But just as he was never to know what he would have done about his love for Lucinda without Fraser's intervention, so he was never to know where his despair would have led him now. Occasionally he thought later it would have killed him. (More often he thought that it would, eventually, have retreated; but retreated as a sea in flood retreats; leaving the land behind it a salty, ruined waste.) However, once again, when he could think of no way out of his predicament, something happened to alter the course of events. And this time what happened was so unexpected, so dramatic, as to transform his despair, in a matter of seconds, into near ecstasy. It wasn't quite ecstasy—there were too many unanswered questions for the transformation to be that complete—but it wasn't far from it; and was, in any case, a wonderful change from the misery he had felt before.

On the morning of the last Saturday in May he received a telegram; and when he opened it, read the following: 'Arrive London Sunday 28 Pan Am Please meet I love you Lucinda.'

To begin with, though his despair did leave him instantly, he couldn't believe it. At least, he told himself he couldn't; what he meant was the shock was too great for the information to be assimilated all at once. She was coming. She was coming! He had been wrong. She hadn't disappeared forever into the darkness that was Fraser. Nor was she standing by Fraser to keep him from that darkness. She loved *him*, and was coming to *him*! He stood at the front door of the cottage with the telegram in his hand, looked at the glowing morning garden—and saw that it had returned to glory. He walked out into that garden, gazed down the street—and saw that the village had become again the kind old place he had always known. He smelled the soft spring air, he heard the birds, he looked up at the round green hills where he had walked as a boy with his father—and wanted to cry out to them that he was back, that he was once more part of them, that once more he *was* them. He felt the ground beneath his feet opening and absorbing him; he felt the whole community stretching out towards him, and embracing him.

Oh Lucinda, he wanted to cry now, in a tone very different from that in which he had cried so recently, you have saved me. You have saved us all.

He spent the next few hours in a state of exaltation, just wandering round and touching things as if he had been blind, and now could see again; and would have spent the whole day in such a state if he hadn't, around five o'clock, had to take first a bus, and then a train, in order to be in London that night, and at the airport early next morning.

But when he was on the train those unanswered questions began to loom up within him: and he began to dwell on the aspects of the affair that had been in the back of his mind, and had worried him, ever since the telegram had arrived.

The first thing he asked himself was why he hadn't heard a word from Lucinda for so long. Before, when they hadn't written to each other, he had rightly perceived of their silence as being no more than a pause in their dialogue. But the silence of the past month hadn't been a pause at all; it had been a sudden, unnatural interruption. Then, even if Lucinda, for reasons of her own, hadn't wanted to be in touch—why had he heard no more from Fraser? The man, knowing him, must also have known how anxious he would be feeling. And not to attempt to allay those anxieties was unFraserlike, to say the least. . . . The third question that Andrew asked himself—and the question which, not knowing the answer to, really made him tremble—was what Lucinda and Fraser had been doing together for all this time. It was just possible of course that Fraser had left San Francisco, as planned, after only a few days, that he and Lucinda hadn't met again, and that the girl had been busy ever since preparing for her own departure. But somehow, not having heard from either of them, he didn't believe this was, or had been, the case. He was certain in fact that Fraser had *not* gone north, that he had remained in San Francisco, and that the two of them had seen each other again. And again and again and again. . . .

He tried to tell himself that even if he were right it didn't matter, since Lucinda was coming to him anyway. It was him she loved. But he couldn't convince himself. Because there was something about the very manner of the girl's arrival that was disquieting. It was too precipitate, too, almost, hysterical. Why hadn't she written to him and said she was thinking of coming? Why hadn't she asked *him* to come to *her*? And why, even if she had decided to come on the spur of the moment, had she written in that telegram 'I love you.' It pleased him, naturally. But it was as if she wanted to reassure him, to dispel any suspicion he might have that she didn't. And why should she think he needed this reassurance, or felt suspicious, if she hadn't given him reason to? Maybe she considered her mere silence such a reason; but maybe, there again, she had given him reason. . . .

It was all, he thought as he sat in his compartment, very very strange. Still, he didn't feel the panic he had been stricken with when imagining what Fraser and Lucinda might do, or become, to each other—he had no cause to; if something *had* happened between them the fact of the matter was that he, as it were, had won—and however much he fretted he was nevertheless able to tell himself, with *almost* complete conviction, that ultimately the only important thing was that tomorrow Lucinda would be here. If he still felt disturbed tomorrow, he was sure she would be able to set his mind at rest.

He spent most of that night worrying about more down-to-earth things—such as whether, though he had no doubt he would love Lucinda all the more when he saw her in the flesh, she might not be disillusioned when she saw him; or whether, after two days in the country, she might not become bored—and by six o'clock was up, shaved, and ready, hours early, to go to the airport. It promised, he saw from the window, to be a beautiful day.

The plane was on time, the passengers didn't take unduly long to collect their bags and pass through customs, and Lucinda was neither the first nor the last of these passengers to emerge into the arrivals hall. She came out surrounded by a group of elderly check-jacketed men carrying golf-bags, and though Andrew had no real idea of what she looked like, as soon as he saw her he knew who she was; as she immediately knew who he was. They smiled at each other tentatively, ruefully, in the manner of a couple who have been living together for years, and want to apologize for a separation that had been long over-extended; then, the final barrier passed, they shook hands. Lucinda raised her eyebrows as if to say 'Well here we are, this is it, though I can't quite believe it still', and Andrew, taking the larger of her two cases, murmured shyly 'Welcome to London.'

Exchanging glances—in order to be sure that each was feeling as amused, as happy, and as afraid as the other; afraid of striking, at the start, the wrong note?—but without another word passing between them, they went, Andrew hesitantly leading, in search of a taxi.

By the time they had reached the flat however—where, Andrew planned, they would stay either until late afternoon, if Lucinda wanted to sleep for a while, or where they would stay just long enough for her to take a shower, have some breakfast, and prepare herself for the last leg of the journey, to the cottage—the ice, if with great caution on both sides, had been broken. ('I feel as if I had just stepped into a room crammed with delicate objects, where one false move could bring the whole lot crashing down.' 'I feel more that I have just started some new story which, unless I get the beginning absolutely right, is never going to work.' 'It better had—I didn't come all this way just to be a couple of lines, then torn up and thrown away.' 'Did you have a good flight?' 'Yes. I was sitting next to some woman who was convinced the plane was going to crash. Every time there was the slightest movement she said "Oh God, Charlie, what's happening?"' 'Who was Charlie?' 'I don't know. She was alone.') And by the time Lucinda had had her shower and her coffee—she didn't want to sleep now; she was eager to get to the country as quickly as possible—Andrew was feeling, though still intensely nervous, even happier than he had hoped he would feel; happier than he could ever remember feeling. Often in the past he had had the sensation of burning with a deep rich flame, as if lit from within by a golden autumn sun. Now he had the sensation of blazing, as if lit, from both within and without, by a dazzling mid-summer sun.

The dream, he told himself, had become reality. . . .

Lucinda was not exactly as he had pictured her. For one thing, though she had said in one of her letters she was tall, she was in fact very tall; far taller than he had expected. For another he had decided that everything about her would be, in the fashion of some nineteenth-century heroine, somehow exquisite; almost, he recalled with a shiver of embarrassment, and a self-deprecating wince—polished to the point of preciousness. Whereas there wasn't, in the actual living person, a trace of preciousness; nor, he told himself with relief, of 'the exquisite'—with all that that word implied in terms of over-refinement, artificiality, and uselessness. She was rather a big-boned, if slim girl, with large practical hands, a wide mouth, and grey direct eyes. Her blonde hair, far from hanging sleekly, silkily from her head, was a thick heavy mane tied loosely at the back of her neck by a twisted elastic band. Her voice, though quiet, wasn't in any way, soft, or weak, or

studied. And her manner, which he had wrong-headedly con-
ceived of as being slightly dreamy, not to say verging on the
mystical (the manner of some only half-human goddess, who
floated an inch or two off the ground), was instead as practical
as her hands, as generous as her mouth, and as direct as her
eyes.

But in spite of all these minor discrepancies (though if
Lucinda had been as Andrew had pictured her he would
probably, he realized with another shiver of embarrassment,
not have been able to bear her), she was just as wonderful in
her entirety as he had wished her to be; if not more so. And
when, that evening, the two of them, without either seemingly
making a conscious effort, moved into each other's arms as
easily and naturally as Lucinda had moved into the cottage—
she had fitted the place, and it had fitted her, as if she had
lived there all her life—he told himself that not only did he
love her; but that whatever difficulties they might have in
the future, of whatever nature, he would never be separated
from her again; even if it meant travelling to the ends of the
earth. He had found his companion. . . .

So passionately and frequently did Andrew tell himself this
over the next few days, and so totally at one did he feel with
Lucinda, that it never occurred to him the girl might not feel
the same. What was more, there was no reason why it should
have occurred to him, since Lucinda seemed as happy and
contented as he was. They really were, Andrew thought, like
a couple who had always known each other, and had merely
been separated for a short, and now inconsequential period.

However, at the end of their first week together (a week
during which they had wandered round the village, gone for
long walks, visited some neighbouring towns and villages,
listened to music, talked, and spent a good deal of time in
bed), while Andrew was as much in love with Lucinda as
ever, and she, he was sure, with him, he became aware that

occasionally, when he glanced at her, he would find her looking thoughtful, or even worried; and aware, too, that the dazzling sun by which he felt himself lit was becoming, if only imperceptibly for the moment, obscured by a mist. And realizing why this mist had risen within him, he guessed the cause of Lucinda's thoughtfulness. They both in fact had the same source; and that source was—it had to be—Fraser.

They hadn't, not once, mentioned the man. He might never have existed; or they might never, before Lucinda had arrived, have known a soul in common. This silence had been, on Andrew's part, half a conscious decision—he hadn't wanted anything ugly to intrude upon his bliss—and half an unconscious decision; he had at times simply forgotten Fraser, so enraptured had he been. But now, he told himself, he could forget about him no longer, and must face the truth; however ugly. Because having been bottled up for so long, the vapours of suspicion were beginning to escape.

Even then, though, it was another three days before he could bring himself to do it; and he would have put it off still longer if it hadn't seemed to him that Lucinda was looking increasingly worried; and that the constantly thickening mist was starting to obscure not only the brightness of his sun, but also its warmth.

He did it one evening, over dinner, and he tried to sound light-hearted; saying 'Oh, that reminds me, what did you make of Fraser?' But almost as soon as he had done it, he knew he shouldn't have; sound light-hearted, that is. For Lucinda, sensing his uneasiness, took advantage of it, and became evasive herself. She smiled, said casually, 'I told you in my letter, he gave me vertigo and struck me as being dangerous,' and then went on to talk about what they were going to do tomorrow.

Which, Andrew felt, was more appalling than the story of a brief affair with the man would have been. That would have stung him, hurt him; but would also have enabled him to tell himself that it was of no consequence; that it was over. But that Lucinda should so refuse to meet him at all, so attempt to dismiss him, could only mean that what was worrying her was too terrible to tell; and was, furthermore, not a thing of the past. It was a thing very much of the present. And of the future, too? Yes, he thought miserably. Of the future. . . .

He respected the girl's reticence of course, admired her for it, and loved her all the more for it; she clearly wanted to spare him what he had come to think of as 'the horror'. And he forced himself to smile back at her, suggest they take a bus to the coast in the morning, and then go on to discuss the possibility of bathing. But as he did he couldn't help shivering; and telling himself that however much he should continue to respect Lucinda's desire to sort out by herself whatever had to be sorted out, he was afraid he wouldn't be able to. He was afraid, very afraid, that he would feel compelled—either tonight, or tomorrow—to return to the subject. If only so he could help her to bear her burden; or if only to know the worst, and not imagine that worst to be more dreadful than it obviously was.

In the meantime he would start to regret that he had raised the matter at all—if he hadn't, unnatural though it might have been, and frightening for a while, eventually the mist would have cleared, and Lucinda's worries died down—and continue to regret that having raised it, Lucinda hadn't given him some sort of satisfaction; hadn't told him something—anything—less disturbing than nothing.

In fact he managed to hold his tongue for another two days. Then, feeling that the mist had become a fog, and was indeed chilling, and that he would be driven mad by Lucinda's now very curious efforts *not* to appear worried, he gave up the struggle.

67

This second conversation—if the first had been a conversation at all—took place on the edge of a wood he had wanted to show Lucinda; a beech wood he had always loved, on the top of a hill with a view of fields and hamlets, a distant cathedral and the sea. And it was in part the very beauty of the place—especially on this June afternoon, with the sky blue, the larks singing, and the trees rustling and silver and bright—that made him suddenly determine to come to terms, once and for all, with the ugliness of his thoughts; and made him equally suddenly, as he was holding Lucinda's hand, plop down on a grassy mound, look up at the tall shining girl in whose hair he had threaded flowers, and say, with an earnestness and mournfulness he couldn't disguise, 'Will you please tell me about Fraser.'

He thought, for a moment, that Lucinda was once again going to fob him off with a smile—a light 'Fraser? What do I know about Fraser?'—and decided that if she did he would tell her of all his doubts and fears and suspicions, and beg her to comment on them, or deny they had any justification, one by one. But (seeing this decision on his face?) Lucinda did not smile—at any rate she checked the smile she had been about to give—and remained motionless, gazing over his head at the trees.

He had to squint to see her, for she was standing against the sun.

She waited for a long time before she spoke; as if her words were clothes, and she had to choose which ones to pack before setting off on a journey. Finally however she was ready; she had selected her outfit.

'I'm probably asking too much of you,' she said, still standing, still gazing at the trees. 'In fact I'm probably asking the impossible. But you must try to give me what I want.'

She paused then; for so long that Andrew carefully, as if afraid of disarranging her neatly packed case, made himself murmur 'I will if I can, but I don't know what you do want.'

'You must try,' Lucinda went on eventually, without apparently having heard him, 'not to ask me for a month. Just for a month. At the end of a month I'll tell you everything. I promise.'

Andrew stared at her as best he could, and didn't move until she slowly lowered herself onto her knees, took a flower from her hair, and started, distractedly, to weave it into his own brown English thatch. Then he took one of her hands, and kissed the palm.

'Why?' he whispered.

Lucinda looked up at the trees again; and again was silent for a long time.

'Because I can't help feeling that if you do ask me you're going to put everything in jeopardy.' Another pause. 'No, *you're* not. *We* are going to put everything in jeopardy. Or just—everything is going to be put in jeopardy.'

She sat down beside him, and looked now into his eyes. She looked steadily, unblinkingly, with a greater seriousness and simplicity than Andrew had ever seen; with such seriousness and simplicity that he couldn't, after a few seconds, bear her gaze any longer, and lowered his head.

Lucinda stroked his hair; he squeezed the hand he was still holding; and both of them spoke, very quietly, at the same time.

Lucinda said 'Please, Andrew.'

Andrew said 'I'll try.'

Then neither of them moved for a while; until, as if they had been rehearsed, they rose together and started to walk, slowly, into the wood.

Andrew did try, for the next ten days; and Lucinda helped him by studying maps with him, reading about various countries with him, and generally trying to distract him with endless talk of where and when their first trip abroad should be. (She also, frequently, asked him to advise her as to what she was going to do with her life. 'I can't just be your travelling companion, can I?' 'I don't see why not. I'd pay you well, and it'd be more interesting than most jobs, I think. Unless there is something else you specifically want to do. In which case you should do it.' 'That's the problem. I don't think there is. Or if there is, I don't know what it is. I mean eventually I want to have a child or two; only that's something else, isn't it?') But though he tried, and though Lucinda did everything in her power to take his mind off Fraser—even saying in desperation one morning 'Look, let's just go away tomorrow. Anywhere. It doesn't matter. Let's just *leave*'—Andrew knew that he was going to fail; that Lucinda *had* asked the impossible of him.

Because just as, a few months ago, Lucinda had come to obsess him, so now Fraser came to obsess him. He felt that the man was continually walking by his side like a baleful ghost; accusing him, threatening him, and standing between him and Lucinda. Fraser ate with them, Fraser was present at their discussions, Fraser lay in bed with them—and with every second that went by Andrew found it harder and harder to avert his eyes from his haunting presence. And the more he stared the more he was certain that, behind Fraser, Lucinda was slipping away. If he did wait a month, he told himself, by the time he finally struck down that ghost Lucinda might have disappeared completely. She had said that if he pressed her he might put everything—by which she clearly meant their relationship—in jeopardy. But by not pressing her, Andrew became convinced, he was putting it in far greater jeopardy. He was even ensuring its end.

Lucinda herself must have realized this; because at the end of those ten days, when he did return, for the third and last time, to the subject of Fraser, in spite of her previous pleas for silence she was ready, without any hesitation now, to meet him.

She didn't hesitate; but she did lay her arms over the atlas she had been looking at, she did lay her head on her arms—and she did look, and sound when she spoke, defeated. . . .

'I met Fraser that first time, as I told you—and as he told you. The day after he called me and asked if we could meet again. We did. We met three more times after that. Then we both knew we mustn't see each other any more. Otherwise we would have betrayed you. I don't mean by that we would have gone to bed with each other—though we probably would have—but that we would have betrayed our friendship, our love of you, and the trust you had placed upon us. In other words I was afraid that if I saw Fraser again I was going to fall in love with him. And I mean fall, almost literally. The only trouble was that Fraser had already taken that step—had already fallen. Or had already clung to me, to stop himself falling. If you see what I mean. We didn't see each other again, though we spoke on the phone a couple of times. Eventually I knew I had to get out. Because even though I hadn't actually met you, I loved you. And I didn't want to love someone else. So I bought my ticket and sent you that telegram. I called Fraser to say goodbye, and he said he would wait for six weeks in San Francisco—just in case things didn't work out between the two of us. He said that if I wasn't back within six weeks he would leave for the north.'

Quietly, Andrew murmured 'Is that all?'

'No, that's not all. And there's no point in being coy about this, or pretending that I'm just being vain. If I don't go back within six weeks Fraser won't leave for the north. He'll kill himself. He didn't say that, he didn't imply that, he didn't even hope I would understand that. But he will, I know. As you must know if you're close to him. He'll kill himself because rightly or wrongly he saw me as either his last chance,

71

or his first chance. Probably both. I told him I would write to him, to let him know one way or the other. I haven't yet.'

Andrew closed his eyes. 'And when you do, what will you tell him?'

Then at last Lucinda did hesitate; and her voice, when she replied, was even quieter than his.

'I don't know. I dare not write.'

Andrew thought of Fraser, waiting in San Francisco. Of his oldest and closest friend. He felt sick. 'If you do go back you won't fall. You'll save him. He'll be able to cling to you, and you'll be able to hold him. You're the first person who ever could. You'd be happy together.'

Lucinda gave what sounded like a brief, sad laugh.

She said: 'Do you think it's possible to love two people?'

'Yes—and no. Not really. Not—'

'No, nor do I. But—I do love you. And I could love him.'

After a moment Andrew whispered, his eyes still closed, 'It's a form of blackmail.'

'No it's not. If I did go back it wouldn't be because I wanted to save his life. It would be because I wanted to love him, and to live with him, and be happy with him.'

'If I asked you to go, if I—sent you back—would you go? If I told you I didn't love you?'

'I don't know. Maybe, if I believed you. But—I don't know.'

'I wouldn't die if you left me. I would be unhappy—desperate—whatever—for a year. Two years. Five years. I would regret your going always. But I wouldn't kill myself. I couldn't. I love life too much. I love England too much.' He paused. 'I want to travel too much.'

'I know.'

Another minute of silence, then: 'Why did you come? You didn't know me. Our love was just a fantasy. A story we'd both made up. Why didn't you just stay, and write me that you weren't coming. You owed me nothing. You had a chance

72

of certain happiness, and you threw it over for—a doubtful dream.'

'The dream's come true.'

'Has it?' Andrew murmured miserably, and opened his eyes.

Eyes which Lucinda must have sensed were open; for she raised her head, and met them.

'Yes,' she said, 'it has.' She turned and looked across the low-beamed, Indian-carpeted room, which was bright and hazy with the late afternoon sun. 'Do you really want to know why I came? Because if I had stayed with Fraser we would have settled down in some small house together—near here probably—which we would never have left again, and all my energy would have gone on trying to hold Fraser up.'

'But if you were happy?'

Lucinda sighed. 'Oh happiness, love,' she said wearily. 'I wanted to travel, like you. That's why I came.' She gave a tiny, rueful smile; the smile she had given when they had first seen each other, at the airport. 'I always used to tell myself when I was small that I was hungry for life.' She shrugged, and looked once more at Andrew. 'I think maybe I'm greedy.'

She waited, then, for him to speak; when he didn't she continued so softly he could hardly hear her. 'So are you. That's why you won't send me away. Though you'd like to, and think you ought to. But you won't. You want the whole world. So you can *know*. So you can tell the whole truth. So you can write better stories, and feel you're doing your bit for humanity—striking a blow for life. And you *will* write better stories. And Fraser,' she concluded, 'will die.'

She was no longer beautiful, Andrew thought; she was, as Fraser had said in his letter, magnificent. She was also, he thought—as Fraser perhaps had meant—terrible. She was as terrible, in her way, as he was. . . .

73

They sat staring across the table for almost five minutes, without saying another word. At the end of that time they stood up, and put their arms around each other.

'I'll write the letter for you if you like,' Andrew whispered.

Lucinda drew back for a second, as if she wanted to study him, and see for the last time something she would never see again. Then she held him more tightly than ever; and said 'Yes, and I'll sign it.'

Two weeks later, feeling slightly apprehensive, they left London for New York; the first step of a journey that was to take them, they had decided, round the world. They had also decided to leave sooner than originally planned, in order to be out of the country before any news from California could arrive. Either from Fraser, telling them he *was* going north, and sending them his blessing; or from a paper, telling them—something else. . . .

Yet though they were slightly apprehensive about this trip they had embarked on, there was, attendant upon their departure, a sense of anticlimax. As if they both knew that they were bound for disappointment; or as if the whole undertaking were somehow superfluous.

Which, Andrew supposed, as he watched England disappear beneath the clouds, it was. For even if, as he prayed, the news from California were *not* bad, he couldn't help feeling that he and Lucinda had already travelled far enough; and certainly much farther than any plane could take them.

The Modern Master

FROM THE NOVEMBER afternoon outside, he turned to a final contemplation of his life.

He started—reading between the lines, and making a summary in his head—at the beginning.

Walter Drake was born in a big old house in the south of England, the youngest child of a fifty-five-year-old banker father, and of a perpetually hurried, perpetually hurrying forty-five-year-old mother. He was, as his parents told him jokingly when he was small, and accusingly as he grew bigger, a mistake. The youngest of his four brothers and sisters was seventeen years older than him.

Some people accept their mistakes; Mr and Mrs Drake could not. They tried; but for the father the unexpected son was an item on the balance-sheet that didn't and couldn't be made to tally; for the hurrying mother he was an obstacle placed in her path; and she tripped. They did their best for him, naturally, and brought him up to have a great respect— too great a respect—for the traditional virtues; God, the monarchy, and the City. But they never felt, nor could make him feel, that he was a natural member of the family. While, therefore, his brothers and sisters were large, loud, hearty creatures, given unreflectingly to tweeds, jolly laughter, and sports of various kinds, he became a grave quiet boy, with the manners of an old man, and a fondness for books about happy children.

He wasn't, however, an unhappy child himself. First, because from the earliest age he somehow understood and sympathized with his parents' feelings towards him; once, on his sixth birthday, he actually apologized to them for the inconvenience his coming had caused. (His father said 'Good heavens, it wasn't your fault'; his mother, wearily, 'That's all right, dear.') Second because he liked his parents; they were both, in the final analysis, good-natured; and if they didn't precisely mean well, they did well enough. And third, and most important, he was happy because while he felt something of an outcast in his own family, and perhaps neither loved nor was loved by his mother or father, he did love, and believed he was loved by, nature. He had a passion for trees and birds, for clouds and hills, that gave him a sense of security, a sense of mutual belonging, that was so intense he never confessed it to anyone, for fear of being told he was silly, or presumptuous. He would spend hours at a time gazing at a single branch, learning its form, taking in its texture, and feeling that as he was part of it, so it was part of him. He would lie on his back in the grass, looking up at the sky, and could be white and billowing, grey and threatening, or just clear and bright and blue, at will. He could fly with swallows, croak with frogs, run through fields with rabbits. What was more, swallows, frogs and rabbits could become, if they wished, a solemn, fair-haired little English boy.

The only part of nature he had difficulty identifying with was the human race.

Inevitably, perhaps, given his background, the excessive conservatism that was drummed into him as a child—all that was old, and fixed, was good—or the fact that he did feel closer to nature than to his parents, he lost, at a comparatively early age, that respect for authority which had been so pronounced till then. The version of reality which those closest had imposed upon him was ultimately too far removed from his own young view of things.

The actual occasion for this loss of faith was—he was always, in later years, to be sure—a fairly trivial incident that occurred when he was eleven; though it didn't seem trivial at the time.

He was lying in bed in the dormitory of the school to which his parents had sent him, waiting for the headmaster to pass, as he did every night, and wish him, and the three other boys in the room, a good night. This particular evening, however, when the tall, red-cheeked, beak-nosed man opened the door, he didn't say what he normally said, or do what he normally did. Instead, he came into the large chilly dormitory, sat down on the edge of Walter's bed, and murmured, obscurely, 'Well, Drake, what do you have to say for yourself?'

Walter, who had nothing to say for himself, blushed, and felt the beginnings of panic.

'Nothing, sir.'

'I saw you, you know.'

Saw him do what? Talking to a flower? Becoming a squirrel? Doing something else he shouldn't have done? Walter didn't know; and unable to reply, blushed deeper.

'You've started young, I must say.'

Walter looked round the room, at the other boys. They seemed as uncomprehending, and apprehensive, as he was.

'I don't know what you mean,' he managed to stammer.

The headmaster leaned forward. He had thick black hair in his nostrils and ears; and his cheeks were purple, not red.

'No? Well, what were you doing in the garden this afternoon?'

That was it then. It was a sin to love nature as he did.

'Nothing, sir,' he whispered, as tears came into his eyes.

'Nothing? You were doing nothing, with my daughter? But I saw you.'

With the man's *daughter*. Ah, Walter thought. . . . The tall thin woman lived near his eldest brother. She had been visiting her father for the day. She had seen Walter, and having met him a couple of times when he was staying with his brother, had stopped him to ask how he was.

'I—'

'You what? You were making proposals to her, I'll be bound.'

Walter shivered. He didn't know what all this was about; but he did know that the headmaster's breath smelled stale, and that his teeth were stained.

'What sort of proposals?'

'Ah, you tell me.'

'I—I don't know.'

'Well, think,' the man suddenly roared. 'What sort of proposals do boys generally make to girls?'

Walter's panic became terror; he started to cry openly. Apart from anything else, the headmaster's daughter wasn't a girl, and hadn't been one for years. She was a thin, nervous woman. . . .

'I don't know,' he repeated.

'You don't know! He doesn't know!' (This to the other boys.) 'Don't talk nonsense. Of course you know. I expect you made some filthy suggestions.'

Walter pressed back against his pillow, and started shaking his head from side to side. This was a nightmare he was having.

'You probably told her you wanted to feel inside her blouse.'

Stop it, the boy wanted to shout. But he just shook his head harder, and felt the tears now spout from his eyes.

'You probably told her you wanted to put your hand up her skirt.'

Stop it—

'Or you wanted to go into the bushes with her—'

Stop it—

'Kiss her—'

Stop it—

'Take your trousers down—'

78

Stop it—
'Didn't you?'
Stop it—
'Didn't you?'
Stop it—
'Answer me!'

'No,' Walter screeched, his voice high and hysterical. 'No,' he sobbed. 'Stop it stop it stop it.'

'Stop it? Stop it? Who do you think you're talking to?'

But Walter could say no more; and shaking, out of control, feeling he were being sucked down into a loathsome bog, he simply waited for some blow to fall on him; some physical attack from this purple-faced madman with his stinking breath.

No blow fell however. For the headmaster suddenly looked around the room, made a strange, choking sound, gave a stranger smile, and, standing up, said hoarsely to the other boys 'Well, he didn't take it too badly, did he?'

Walter's school-fellows stared.

The man looked back at Walter. 'I was only teasing, you know. I wanted to see if you could take a joke. A chap's got to be able to take a joke, you know.'

Walter didn't speak. He couldn't have if he'd wanted to, and he didn't want to. It had all been a joke. . . .

Except it hadn't been, and the boy continued to cry for another half hour; long after the headmaster had said goodnight, and had turned out the light.

When he stopped crying he told himself that he would never trust that man again. Furthermore, he came to think over the next year or two, since headmasters were in league with fathers, politicians, judges and bishops—were part of a brotherhood that decided what was true; a brotherhood of the old, and so-called wise—he would never trust any of them again. Neither them, nor their truths.

He didn't; and as a result it was perhaps even more inevitable that sooner or later (it happened in fact when he was sixteen) he should go all the way, and lose his faith in the ultimate fount of truth: God. Though this final loss of faith was not occasioned by any particular incident; merely by his inability, when he had thought about it long and hard, and when he had looked at the world about him, to see any evidence whatsoever for the existence of a deity.

'Even if there were proof,' he told a friend, 'I wouldn't want anything to do with Him.'

Yet if the taking of the step was undramatic, the results of it, for a while, were less so. For Walter had been brought up to believe that the entire structure of civilization was built upon the foundation of God. To have questioned that structure—and, by now, found it wanting—was one thing; but to see the foundation disappear as well was almost too much. It made the boy feel shattered; feel that the earth had slipped away beneath his feet; that he were falling into space.

For four years he reeled through life, trying to find something to hold on to. Finding nothing—though devoting all his energy to the search—he led, at least outwardly, the same existence he would have led if he had lost nothing. That is, he finished school, went up to Oxford, and spent most of his free time taking walks in the country, and studying wildlife.

At the end of four years, however, he pulled himself together, and lost his fear of falling. Or rather, he stopped falling; and saw that essentially his loss of faith was irrelevant. For aside from the fact, of which he became fairly certain, that civilizations would have grown and developed even without gods, he realized that if he had lost his faith in the accepted, the authorized version of reality—in the stories that men invented to make the world bearable (and, incidentally, to bolster the authority of fathers, headmasters, and politicians) —he had in no way lost his faith in the reality of the natural world. Indeed, he reasoned, that was the only reality; and men's actions could only be explained in terms of it.

Having pulled himself together, he began to wonder what he was going to do with his future.

It took him several more years to find an answer to this question; and during these years he abruptly left Oxford (deciding that it was merely a pulpit from which the brotherhood he more and more rejected preached), travelled as widely as he could, and supported himself by doing a variety of jobs.

Then, at the age of twenty-six, he was ready.

Since people liked fictions, he would, he told himself, become a novelist. He would write books that, hopefully, challenged the very notion of fiction; of what was true, and what was not. Books that suggested, if only by implication, that were people to question their own reality, they would be less likely to become victims of their own, or other people's, dreams. And—most optimistically—books that proclaimed that if only people would see themselves as an integral part of a vast whole—of the natural world—without in any way being special, or particular, they would not only be happier, but would also make that world a finer place to live in. (Why people saw themselves as somehow set above and apart from the natural world, and why they had invented gods, was, he maintained, because man alone of all animals was conscious of his own death; and was afraid of it. It was that fear which caused him to seek the eternal, the immutable; it was that fear which caused him to retreat into greed and cruelty, egoism and falsity; and it was that fear which, by making him embrace the dead and cold, *did* set him apart from the natural world.)

Having made his decision, and having only added, to himself, that all mankind, and each individual, could be divided into wiseman and fool—the wiseman being he who did view himself as merely a part of the whole, who realized that any hurt he did to his fellow man, or to the world around him, was a hurt to himself, and who chose, consciously, his own reality; the fool being he who thought man entire in himself, who believed that he had to dominate the world, his fellows and himself, and who led, as it were, the life that others had written for him—he got down to work, and embarked upon his career.

That it was the right career he felt certain after he had finished his first book. For he sensed that by writing it, by—as he perceived it—denying himself, and offering himself as an instrument upon which the world could play (his beliefs being just the strings of that instrument), he had managed at last to become one not only with trees and animals, but also with his fellow men. He was no longer the youngest son, the mistake; he was indeed a part of the whole.

Over the next twenty years he devoted his life to his work, turning out a novel a year, and—in his constant striving to become ever more integrated, in his constant desire to reject, as far as he could, the illusions which destroyed other men (to reject, in other words, the part of himself that was a fool)—attempted to eliminate everything that was not work, or work connected, from his daily routine. He had to make compromises of course—for instance, he distrusted possessions, and thought the longing for possessions foolish; yet knowing he needed peace and security in order to write well, he accepted the small legacy his father left him, and bought a house, set in a large overgrown garden, in West London—but at least when he did so he was aware they were compromises; and worked all the harder afterwards to compensate for them.

In fact the only real dilemma he had to face was whether to marry, or, more particularly, whether to have children. A part of him held that he should—that, surely, was in the natural scheme of things—but another part, and ultimately the stronger part—told him that believing as he did that his work was the great thing that bound him to the earth, he should reserve himself entirely for that work, since only by doing so could he, personally, be happy. And being happy meant, for him, being good; and being good, being true to the earth; to life.

He contented himself therefore—possibly because he too, in a corner of his brain, was afraid of death, and the separateness that the knowledge of death caused men to feel—by having the occasional affair, generally with brown-toned, brainy women who worked in publishing companies, or who taught—and by telling himself that should he ever decide to retire he could, if it weren't too late, always revise his opinions, and change his mind. After all, there was no reason why he shouldn't marry at fifty, or sixty; nor, if he married a younger woman, have children. And he was sure that if he did decide to he would find someone to accept him. Because it wasn't as if he were physically repulsive, or lived as a hermit. On the contrary, what with lunches, and dinners, and the occasional party, with weekends spent in the country, and trips abroad twice a year, he led what many would have considered quite a social life; and therefore came into contact with a great many people. (He did this principally to gather material for his books, to harvest the grain to make the bread he hoped would nourish the world. Nevertheless it did keep him in practice, as far as social relations were concerned.)

Not that he seriously thought, in those first twenty years of his career, that he ever would give up writing. And when, at the age of forty-six, he started to consider the possibility, it *was* already too late. For the retiral he contemplated was definitive.

He had had, as all men did, periods of dejection throughout his life; periods when it seemed that everything he did was useless, that he wouldn't, however well he worked, however clearly his note rang out, be able to change a thing in this sad universe. (He didn't expect to change the course of history; but he did hope that his words might touch one or two people; one or two who would become three or four, then three or four who would become—well, a number.) But generally these moods didn't last very long, and he was able to dismiss them—and their attendant feelings of boredom, and frustration—by seeing them for what they were: i.e. attacks of egoism, attacks of the illusion that *he* was set apart from, set above the natural order of things.

But when he was in his mid-forties, imperceptibly at first, and then overwhelmingly, a sense of hopelessness settled over him that he couldn't shake off, despite all his efforts to view it as mere egoism; as a mere longing, on the part of the youngest son, not only to be included in the family, but to dominate it.

It had, this awful sense, just one cause. His books were not successful. That is to say, though they sold in quantities sufficient to make their publication commercially viable, and though they were nearly all well received by critics, they did not, as their author not only wished them to be, but believed they should, become widely read, indeed popular; and worse, all, without exception as far as he could tell, were read, whether by critics or such public as they had, only as stories, without any understanding or perception of what those stories signified. (Though how this was possible he wasn't sure; for it seemed to him that unless the portraits he painted were viewed in the particular light he shone upon them they must be invisible; or anyway formless, colourless, and ugly.) Which led him first to the conclusion that if there were anyone at all in the world who did not believe in absolute truths he or she was not among those who bought books, and then—as his hopelessness really gripped him—to the conclusion that the fool in every man dominated the wiseman, that the fools of the world dominated the wisemen, and that there was no chance of changing this situation, ever.

He tried to reason with himself; tried to tell himself that the man, whether author or not, who felt himself misunderstood was the most common of all mortals, and that, once again, his dejection was just a manifestation of his egoism, and fear. But he couldn't convince himself. First because the fact that he shared his complaint with other men didn't make it any less of a complaint; and second because it wasn't a recognition of himself that he desired, but a recognition of his *denial* of himself. It was his own *lack* of egoism, his warnings against egoism, and his profound belief that only through a renunciation of the greedy frightened self could the world be helped, that he wished to be known.

Having failed on this score, he then tried to combat his gloom by telling himself that it was the nature of his books that prevented them becoming popular. Those books that were, inevitably, about writers (whether actual 'writers', or fishermen, farmers, factory hands), who struggled with the materials available to them, and, in the absence of any set of rules telling them what to do, tried to create good stories of their lives. Perhaps they were too didactic, he told himself. Perhaps they were too elusive, and gave the sense of having been written in a hall of mirrors, so that it was impossible to tell what was real, and what was reflection. (What was fact, and what was fiction.) Or perhaps he had strung himself too tightly, so that the music that emerged from him was harsh, ugly, and difficult to listen to. Maybe if he relaxed a little a sweeter sound would emerge. . . .

There again, he failed. For he had always taken care *not* to be didactic—he had never imposed 'a meaning' upon his books; all that was implied, suggested or proclaimed by them was inherent in the story—just as he had always taken care not to be gratuitously elusive, or ambiguous. And as for stringing himself too tightly—he refuted that charge entirely. If anything, in his determination to deny himself, he hadn't at times strung himself tight enough; so that his music had moments of sloppiness. But it was never harsh or difficult. He had a sufficiently good ear to be sure of that.

No, he decided finally, the real reason for his lack of success was the one his editor had given him when, unable to contain himself any longer, he had told her of his feelings.

'Your books, Walter,' the woman had said, 'are very good. And they could be successful. Very successful, in a limited way. But if you aren't going to write the big, popular best-seller—which you're clearly not, and clearly don't want to—you must fix your name in the public's eye. You must give the world a person, an image, to hang on to. You must, to put it crudely, do some publicity.'

Which was the last straw; and the proof, if any were needed, that fools held sway in the land. Because all his life Walter had abhorred publicity; had thought fame, or the desire thereof, one of the most dangerous of all illusions; and had believed that the seeking of refuge in a public image was one of the clearest illustrations of the way that men sought death in life. He wanted his *books* to be known; not that atom in the universe that was called, for the sake of convenience, Walter Drake. He had always refused to give even the shortest interview; to talk to a representative of even the most obscure magazine. To do so would be unforgivably foolish.

At the age of forty-eight, therefore, he decided to do two things. One was to write, with as much honesty as possible, an autobiography; in the bitter hope, or belief, that a world that had rejected his quick, living body—his novels—would accept a hard dead shell, and take it to be the body; and the still more bitter hope that by betraying his principles, and writing a book that did *not* deny the self—a necessarily sour thin book that would be a catalogue of disappointment, egoism and greed—he would demonstrate for all time the validity of those principles.

The other thing he decided to do—the only thing he could do having so succumbed to his bitterness—was kill himself.

This then was Walter Drake's version of himself. (Other people would have had different versions. One woman he knew had called him 'the worn-out representative of a worn-out class'. Another had called him—having commented on his grey hair, his grey skin, his grey voice, and the grey suits he always wore, 'the most impeccably dull man in London'. And yet another, after he had had a brief relationship with her, had said that his total dedication to his work was nothing but the dedication of a man who is frightened to live—whatever that meant.) And, he thought, as he put down the manuscript, looked at the falling darkness outside, and realized the only remaining task to be done was wrap the thing up and take it to the post-office, it was indeed a sour thin version. Not only sour and thin but, even on its own terms, false. For though he had determined to be honest, there was one fact he had left out of the story. (The story, he repeated to himself, that was, precisely because of the egoism that inspired it, so much less true than his novels.) He had left it out because he wasn't certain just how far it constituted a fact, and because it didn't fit in with the general tone of wretchedness.

This omitted fact, or whatever, of his life, this single, troublingly positive chord in the bleak music of his existence, was a skinny, red-haired Austrian Jewish woman of indeterminate age, whose name was Anna Stein. Or better, since Walter had never called her Anna, plain—Mrs Stein.

He thought of her as he walked through the damp, leaf-strewn streets to the post-office. . . .

Feeling, once his career was underway, that he did now have a part in society, knowing that he needed peace and quiet, and realizing that he must have a fairly regular contact with humanity, he decided that he should live in a town, rather than in the country; and decided, when he saw the house in West London, with its surrounding, overgrown garden, that such a place would be ideal.

Which, having been bought and moved into, it turned out to be—but for one small drawback. It was just too big for him to take care of by himself; or for him to take care of without having household chores waste too many of his working hours. He made, therefore, what he couldn't help thinking of as a further compromise; and put an advertisement in the local newsagent's for a cleaning woman.

Mrs Stein was the second person who answered the advertisement, and as soon as he met her Walter knew that he had found what—who—he was looking for. First because with her bright dyed hair, her skeletal frame, her accent, and her general air of oddness, the woman fitted in with the house; which, with its steeply sloping roof, its low overhanging eaves, its little stained-glass windows, and its four rather precarious floors, was also somewhat odd; and second because he liked the way she told him that if she took the job she couldn't keep regular hours. She would work five days a week, and would stay for as many hours per day as necessary; but she wouldn't (she didn't say why) specify what those hours would be; nor even what those days would be.

She started the following week—on Walter's thirty-fourth birthday—and within a month had convinced the novelist that—as with his career—he had made the right choice. Mrs Stein cleaned for him, she did his laundry, she cooked— depending on what time she came—the occasional meal for him, and she left him in peace. Left him in peace to such an extent that at times he felt obliged to interrupt his work and go to disturb her.

Within a year he was telling himself he wouldn't be able to live without her. . . .

It wasn't only that she did everything for him—including paying his bills, going to the bank, doing his shopping, and dealing with most of his mail—and thus enabled him to concentrate exclusively on his work; she also gave him something he had never had before. Which was warmth.

How she gave it to him he wasn't sure; at the end of that first year she was no more communicative than she had been eleven months before. She called him always—with a note of accusal in her voice—Mr Drake. She only occasionally came to talk to him (though if she wanted something she would march straight into his study, without a thought that she might be halting the flow of his sacred prose, and without a word of apology), and she wasn't always receptive when he wanted to talk to her. (She had the peculiarity of being both hard of hearing, and extremely sensitive to noise; so much so that at times, when he was speaking, she would stop him in mid-sentence, mutter 'I can't listen to you today, Mr Drake,' and dismiss him from her presence.) Above all, she always rejected out of hand the idea that she should read one of his books. 'I don't need books, Mr Drake,' she would say as she sewed, or cooked, or cleaned. 'The world's quite enough for me.'

Yet in spite of all this—though he rather approved of her attitude to his work—give him warmth she did; and gave him, furthermore, the impression that while she didn't want to read his books, while she never seemed curious about his family or private life (did she realize he didn't have one?), and while, when she asked his opinion on something, she received it with an air of scepticism that bordered on contempt, she understood him better than the most perceptive reader of his work could ever have understood him.

This impression was confirmed for him one summer afternoon, when Mrs Stein had been with him for eighteen months. He was sitting in his garden (which had become far more overgrown since he had bought the house, and was—and was to remain for another six years, until he felt obliged to have a gardener once a week—a virtual jungle), wondering whether to have a mug of tea, when the pale, flame-haired woman came out to find him; and told him that since the cost of living had gone up, and since—because she had checked his accounts? —she knew he could well afford it, she was giving herself a raise. 'Of course,' Walter said—not that he could have refused —and asked her if she would like some tea herself. He didn't expect her to say yes, and was almost unreasonably delighted when she did. And when she was sitting in front of him, flapping, with her thin veined hand, at imaginary flies, and looking, for her, fairly benevolent, he decided that now was the time to find out a little more about her. About her age, for example— which he guessed was around forty-five, but could equally have been sixty—about her background, and about whether there was a Mr Stein. She was uncommunicative on the first issue— 'I'm old enough, Mr Drake,' she muttered into her teacup— but on the second and third she was slightly more forthcoming. She had come to England just before the outbreak of the Second World War (as a child? As a teenager? As a young adult?) and had lost all her family—mother, father, two sisters and a brother—in 'one of those places'. She had married (when? Where?) at the age of twenty-one; and her husband had also been an Austrian Jew. He had been a small-time importer exporter; but had invariably imported and exported goods that no one really wanted. She could have run his business much more successfully, but apart from the fact that the mismanagement of his affairs was necessary to him, she had had her own work. She had been a dance teacher. 'I wanted to be a dancer myself when I was young,' she said. 'But things didn't work out like that.' She had taught for a number of years, until two things had happened, more or less simultaneously. One was that the only pupil she'd ever had who'd shown real promise ('Her mother was Austrian, Mr Drake') had, just as her career was about to take off, abandoned it for marriage; thereby disgusting her teacher so much that she had vowed to abandon *her* career; and the other was that Mr Stein had died; leaving his affairs in such a mess they had required two years of constant attention for anything to be salvaged from the ruins. When the estate had finally been settled the widow had supported herself by doing a number of jobs—which she'd always had to leave because of the noise—until she had decided that taking care of a single person's house might be the right solution for her. Soon after she had decided she had seen the advertisement in the newsagent's.

'But do I,' Walter asked, 'pay you enough to live on, even with your raise?'

No, of course not, Mrs Stein said. But she did one or two other things. . . .

'How old was Mr Stein when he died?' Walter asked; hoping thereby to pin the widow down on the subject of her own age.

'He was old enough,' Mrs Stein said.

'What,' Walter asked, lowering his voice, and attempting with his manner to pour balm on a wound even as he poked it, 'did Mr Stein die of?'

'Hatred,' Mrs Stein said, as she broke a flower off an oleander bush, and sniffed at it.

Walter thought that would be the woman's only comment on her husband's decease. But, surprisingly, it wasn't. For having given the poisonous bloom another sniff, she looked at the grave youngish man she worked for, shook her head, and murmured, 'He could never forgive the Fools.'

That she had said Fools, and not mere fools, Walter was instantly certain; as he was certain that, though he had never spoken of his beliefs to Mrs Stein, what she meant by the word Fool was precisely what he meant by it.

For a second, sitting in that overgrown garden, with the bees buzzing about him, and the planes flying overhead, Walter was tempted to stand up, go over to the angular woman in front of him, and embrace her. He found her, suddenly, beautiful. And even when that second had passed—for of course he couldn't embrace her; not because he was afraid she would have rejected him (indeed he was strangely sure she wouldn't have) but because to have done so might have changed the course of his life—he continued to gaze at her in gratitude and admiration, and continued to find her beautiful. Oh, he told himself, he *had* been right. She understood him. She *understood* him!

Though he didn't, for a while thereafter, stop having the occasional brief affair, Walter did, from that day on, make sure that Anna Stein never knew about it; and he did, too, whenever he embraced some other woman, feel that he was betraying his thin, harsh housekeeper. . . .

Why he believed that the woman wouldn't have rejected his advances if he'd made them, was a question he was to ask himself as frequently in the following years as he had formerly wondered how she gave him warmth; and to ask himself with special urgency when, as happened every two or three months, he was tempted not only to put his arms around her, but to ask her to marry him. Yet though he was no more able to find an answer to this question than he had been to that other, and though he often tried to convince himself it was mere wishful thinking on his part, he could never rid himself of his belief. There was just something about the way Mrs Stein looked at him—scornfully, but humorously—something about the way she spoke to him—dismissively, but kindly—and above all something about the way she always called him Mr Drake—he had asked her to call him Walter several times, but she had invariably given a kind of shrug, as if he were asking the impossible of her—that made him feel that for all the difference, whatever it was, in their ages, for all the difference in their characters, and for all their lack of common interests, Mrs Stein both reciprocated his affection, and held him as essential to her life as he held her essential to his.

(They really did have nothing in common, however. He was a quiet retiring man whose considerable passion was entirely directed to his work; she was an acid, rather aggressive woman whose passion, if any, was directed to the dyeing of her hair and the sharpening of her tongue. He liked Mozart; she liked 'light music'. He hated television; she professed to adore it; especially westerns, and soap operas. He, of course, loved nature; she—going almost as far as Miss Stein—told him, when he pointed out a laburnum in the garden one day, 'A tree is a tree, Mr Drake,' and scarcely glanced at the beautiful flowering thing.)

They would have made an odd couple if they had married; and Walter had difficulty in imagining them lying in bed together, going out together, or going on holiday together. (Though maybe they wouldn't have gone on holiday together, since Mrs Stein didn't like leaving London; or even West London.) But for all his difficulty he was convinced that they would have made, nevertheless, a happy couple. Indeed, he told himself, they would have made an ideal couple. . . .

Their relationship continued then, more or less unchanged, for twelve years; until, that is, Walter's great gloom settled over him. When it did, two things happened. One was that the author, who hadn't had any sort of affair, or even sex, for the previous three years, suddenly found his physical attraction to Anna Stein becoming overwhelming—every time he saw her, or just smelled the scent of the soap she used, he wanted not only to embrace her, but to cling to her, to kiss her, and to hold her thin body against his own—and the other was that having despaired of his career, and conceded the field to fools, though he did so want his red-haired housekeeper, he also despaired of his love; and realized that the prospect of individual contentment was barred to him forever.

He made, therefore, at the instant of deciding to write his autobiography, another decision; which was that for the time it took him to complete the book, he would see as little of Mrs Stein as possible.

He locked his study door; he left notes for her; and he ignored, when he did see her, the expression on her face; which was either one of irritation for what she considered his preciousness ('What are you writing, Mr Drake?' she asked mockingly one day. 'A masterpiece?')—or one of deep hurt. ('It's a bit late to decide I disturb you,' she told him, with an attempt at mockery, another day; after she had rattled at his study door for five minutes, and demanded to be let in on the excuse that she had to clean the windows.) He wasn't certain which that expression was; and he tried not to think about it.

The day he finished the first draft of his book—three months ago now—he also went to see his solicitor, and made a will leaving all he possessed to Mrs Stein.

Which would, in some small way, he hoped—as he got to the post-office, and handed over the neatly wrapped manuscript—make up for his having so neglected her in his Life. For his having hardly mentioned her at all—just making the occasional passing reference—and worse, for his having passed over entirely the love he had always felt for her.

Though, he told himself, as he started to walk, for the last time, back towards his house, she probably wouldn't mind his dishonesty—his not having made her one of the facts of his life—too much. For even assuming she read the book—which was a large assumption—she would understand why he had made the omission. She had always understood him. . . .

It was a quarter to five when he reached home; and at five o'clock he was ready for the final deed.

He had hoped, when he was younger, that before he died he would have time to destroy not only all his personal papers, his manuscripts, and his letters, but everything he owned; so that after his death the only thing that remained of him would be his life—his novels. When he had decided to kill himself, and write the autobiography, he had—by leaving behind both his real, unrecognized life, and that other book, which people would take for his real life—modified his ideas a little. But he had modified them in no other way, and his intention of destroying all the rest of the so-called evidence of his existence was as firm as ever.

Which had led him to the conclusion that the best way to end his time on earth was to burn down the house, with himself inside it. This did of course mean that Anna Stein would inherit, in the way of real estate, only a large garden and a pile of ashes; but that, he was afraid, was just one of those things. Besides, the land by itself would be worth a fair amount.

He hoped, when thinking of the precise details of his death, that he would—as he believed was generally the case—be overcome and killed by smoke and fumes, rather than actually burned alive. But even were the worst to happen, he told himself as he went into his study, walked over to the fireplace, and deliberately kicked two large flaming logs on to the hearth-rug—on which he had stacked a number of manuscripts—his agony wouldn't last very long. No more than a couple of minutes, surely. . . .

He left his study, walked out into the wood-panelled hallway, up the staircase to the first floor, and into his bedroom. He lay down on his bed.

He tried, stretched out there, to think of his past; of his parents, of his childhood, of boat rides taken on summer lakes, of walks through the Black Forest. But either because he was too intent on catching the first whiff of smoke from downstairs, or because he had spent the whole day—not to say most of the last nine months—reviewing his past, and had had enough of it, none of the images he sought came to him; and he eventually settled first—as his eyes began to water, and he did at last catch the scent of burning wool, and paper—on a contemplation of the world that he was leaving—the world that had not heeded a voice crying 'There is a way', and was controlled by Fools who were victims, and who made others victims, of their fear and egoism—and after that, on a final but longer contemplation of his feelings for Anna Stein. Why *had* he cared so much for that odd woman? Was it only because he felt that they were each of them, in their different ways, refugees from the reality they had been born into? Or was it because she, so totally different from him in background, temperament, beliefs, was, nevertheless, a kind of physical manifestation of what he felt within? He didn't know. Possibly both these explanations were valid; or possibly neither. Possibly it was just a matter of his being sexually attracted, for whatever reason, to a thin harsh woman somewhat older than himself; or possibly, even—though this was the least pleasant of all the alternatives—that he hadn't actually loved or wanted Mrs Stein at all, and had simply used her idealized presence as an excuse for not committing himself to anyone. . . .

That anything, at this point, could have made him change his mind about what he was doing—or have taken his mind off Anna Stein; whose image, regardless of the explanation of his feelings for her, had the effect on him, as his eyes, throat and nose really began to hurt, of a tranquillizer, or of a gentle calming guide who supported him as he ascended his funeral pyre—never, for a moment, occurred to him. Yet, a very short time later, something did make him change his mind. Though it made him think more than ever of Mrs Stein. . . .

He was, as he had hoped, on the point of losing consciousness. The house, with all its wood, and carpets, and draughts, had really caught. His room was full of smoke, and was very hot. He was coughing, choking. He heard a great noise of cracking and breaking, and of things exploding; and he realized that something peculiar had taken place; the flames had leapt up the stair well, and the top of the house was burning as fiercely as the ground floor. More fiercely, for the moment, than his own floor. Maybe, he thought, as he felt himself sinking into a thick, foul cloud—a cloud that seemed to be emanating from inside him—and as he gasped for the last remaining traces of oxygen in the room, before the floor collapsed, or his bed caught fire, the ceiling would fall on him. . . . It was at this moment that he heard the scream. For just a second he thought he was imagining things—or that the noise had come from outside. But then, as he heard it again, he knew that he hadn't imagined it, that it wasn't coming from outside— and that it was the scream of Anna Stein.

He didn't think; he didn't have to. Mrs Stein, his beloved Mrs Stein, was in the house. She must have come for some reason, though she had told him yesterday that she wouldn't be in today, while he was at the post-office. She must have gone up to the little room on the top floor where she did her sewing and ironing—a little room at the back of the house whose light he wouldn't have seen when he returned. And now she was trapped up there and was, because of him, in danger of being burned to death. Which mustn't happen; which couldn't happen. He had wanted to kill himself, not anyone else. And above all not her. He had to save her. . . .

He didn't know how he got to the window. Nor how, having somehow found it in the smoke, he had the strength—having tried and failed to open it—to smash it with his bare hands, to knock out the jagged pieces of glass, and to climb onto the window ledge. He knew even less how, as he was about to jump from that window ledge, praying that he didn't kill himself in the process, and that the big hydrangea bush beneath would break his fall, he remembered, or saw, that there was a drainpipe running down the side of the house, and he managed to grab it and climb, slide down into the garden. All he did know was that he had to get the ladder that was kept in the garden shed, that he had to put it up against the side of the house, and that he had to save Mrs Stein. He had to save her. . . .

He became aware, as he pulled himself out of the bush, of a number of people standing in the garden, their faces lit by the flames. Some were shouting, some pointing, and one was holding a camera. He became aware of himself shrieking hysterically, though he could hardly form the words, 'Call the fire brigade,' and of someone yelling back 'We have.' He became aware of his rushing, stumbling, staggering to the shed, of his finding other people there already pulling out the ladder, and of their all dragging it to the back of the house; on the top floor of which, leaning out of a small window, screaming and screaming and screaming—Walter hadn't known it was possible to scream in such a way—was Anna Stein. And finally he was aware, after his helpers had extended the ladder, leant it against the house, and been pushed violently aside by him, of his being half, or more than half way up that ladder when above him Mrs Stein, her hair literally flaming now—and her dress too—leaning right out of the window, and giving one more terrible scream, seemed to stretch out a hand towards him—and fell. Or maybe she jumped. . . .

He wasn't sure, when he awoke in hospital next morning with his hands bandaged, what Mrs Stein had done. Nor did the spectacular photograph, that was in every daily newspaper, and on the front page of most—a photograph that showed a middle-aged man, dressed in a grey suit, standing on a ladder with blood running from his hands, reaching out in vain for a thin blazing body, its face contorted with terror, that was falling past him—make the matter any clearer. All he was sure of—and it made the precise nature of the fall unimportant—was that Anna Stein was dead; and that he had killed her.

He had killed her. He had killed her. He told himself this again and again as he lay in his hospital bed. He told himself this as he answered a phone-call—he had been about to call himself—from his publishers, and having listened to their condolences, and to their expressions of relief that he at least was all right, told them that they would, in the next day or two, be receiving a manuscript from him; a manuscript that was under no circumstances to be opened or looked at, and was to be returned instantly to him. He told himself this as he spoke to the police, and recounted how he had gone out to the post-office just before five, how he had walked back to his house, built up the fire in his study, and then, feeling weary, had gone to his bed to rest for an hour or so; and how, woken by the smoke, he had heard Mrs Stein screaming, and had realized she had come in while he had been out. And he told himself this as he spoke to the reporters who besieged the hospital, and he repeated and repeated—which was why he agreed to speak to them; it was the very least he could do for the poor woman's memory—that Anna Stein hadn't 'just' been his housekeeper. She had been far, far more. She had been—and he didn't care how emotional it sounded—the only woman he had ever loved.

Perhaps the tragedy happened in a slow week for news. Or perhaps there was something about it that appealed to newspaper proprietors. The reserved English writer and the refugee. . . . (Ah, and how he learned now the facts of Mrs Stein's life!) Whatever the reason, within a week the story, and again that photograph, had appeared not only in English papers, but in the papers and magazines of half the world. And within a year Walter realized that those logs he had displaced from his hearth had ignited not only his house, but also the hitherto barely warm embers of his reputation. For his publishers, having at last a name to play with, and able to beat effectively on the drums of publicity, had reprinted a number of his books; and had brought them out—because of that publicity?—to greater attention and acclaim than their author had ever dreamed possible. . . .

To such attention and acclaim, indeed, that fairly soon Walter Drake had become something of a cult figure; and was well on his way to being considered a modern master. And as he saw his reputation growing, and the beliefs he had always passionately held being given the dues he thought they deserved, he even, very discreetly, started to lend his own scarred hands to the beating of the drums.

Yet though, by the age of fifty-five, he had attained the position he had aspired to for so long, and though, especially among the young, his ideas had found a fertile ground in which to flourish, he was not, according to his own definition, a happy man.

Nor, he told himself one day, as, after much deliberation, he built a fire in the study of his new house, and threw onto it the manuscript of his autobiography, was he ever likely to be.

For he knew that whatever recognition he received, he would never be able to forget Mrs Stein and what he had done to her; and knew further, that though the world now hailed him as a wiseman, he would always, till the day he died, think of himself as a fool.

The Power of Love?

SHE KNEW WHY HE'D DONE IT; he was asserting his independence. Still, as she put the phone down, she was hurt. Not only because of the story, but also because of the way he had told it. There had been a note of glee in his voice; as if he had known he was hurting her, and had wanted to hurt her.

'Basically it's the story of a rich unattractive woman married to a younger man who plans to kill her to inherit her money and marry the woman he has been having an affair with for years.'

'I imagine,' she had said, 'that the rich unattractive woman's name is Fran, that her husband's name is Gerhard, and the other woman's name is Lucie.'

'Oh, for heaven's sake, Fran,' he had protested, all righteous indignation. 'Stop being paranoid.'

Then he had laughed.

Not for the first time, as she uncurled her little legs from the sofa, got up, and went to find a cigarette, she considered asking him to move; or even evicting him. Of course if she did he would really attack her, really savage her. But at least then she would have the satisfaction of knowing that his attack was that of the abandoned stray; that it was, in a sense, justified. Whereas to be bitten by a creature she had always given shelter to, had fed tid-bits to, and had doted on, would not only bring her no satisfaction, but would make her very wary of ever giving shelter to anyone else. Which would be a terrible state of affairs.

She needed a pet about the place.

Two minutes later, however, having lit a cigarette, having put on a record of some music by a young Polish composer she had just discovered, and having told herself she didn't care that Gerhard, who would be home shortly, would berate her for doing both, she dismissed any such consideration from her mind. For one thing she knew that it was extremely unlikely that David would actually write that story; it wasn't at all his genre. For another she *did* understand him, and realized it *must* be difficult for him to feel dependent on her. And for yet another, she couldn't throw him out because of all the young men and women she had given shelter to in the past, he was the first who promised to be—who already was—something more than a lame dog. He was the first, indeed, who promised to be a champion. . . .

Possibly, though, it was just this sense that she had, almost in spite of herself, picked a winner this time—and therefore couldn't evict him—that made Fran feel, when Gerhard did come in, and she told him, as casually as she could, the plot of the book that David Chezzel was proposing to write, more hurt than ever. Not only hurt but also, absurdly, frightened. If it was *not* because of this, it was because after Gerhard, looking both angry and amused, had listened to her, he had told her that she knew he couldn't stand to be in the house if she'd been smoking, or if she were playing her squeaks and bumps—and had gone out again.

As he had left he had called, with a laugh, 'I think David's story is quite good. Though God knows why *you're* helping him to write it.'

It had been a ridiculous thing to say, Fran told herself as she went to bed at eleven. (Gerhard wasn't back yet.) Still, she hadn't been able to help repeating it to herself all evening as she waited for her husband, made dinner for Cyrus, and thought again and again of that story; and couldn't help repeating it to herself now as she lay alone between the sheets.

Obviously in one way she knew why she was helping David; it was for the same reason she had helped all those others. She was (trying to see herself objectively) a small, plump, unattractive, middle-aged woman, who was extremely wealthy and reasonably intelligent. Yet though she was intelligent, hers was an analytical intelligence, a critical intelligence. It was not a creative intelligence. She could see through anything; discern its nature, its texture, its composition. She could also see through anyone, herself included. Her vision of the world was, she liked to think, unclouded by rhetoric, sentimentality, or guilt. Or—she liked to think more—by meanness, greed or pettiness. Some of her friends summed her up by saying she had great taste; others by saying she was happy. Both in a way were true; yet they were both terms she dismissed as largely meaningless. She had taken account of the cards she had been dealt; and played with them as best she could. That was all there was to it. And one of the cards she hadn't been dealt was imagination. She could cope with the facts as she saw them, and she saw them exceptionally clearly; but she couldn't cope with facts, or even conceive of facts, that she didn't see. Realizing this quite early on, and realizing equally that imagination was a force that had to be reckoned with—without imagination there would be no music, no paintings, no plays, no books (all the things, in other words, that served to make reality understandable to her)—she determined to do something to encourage the growth of this flower that was not in her own garden. And caring more for books than for any other form of art—and owning, amongst other things, an apartment building in the West Seventies—she had, from the age of twenty-six onwards, kept three rooms in this building free for writers who needed somewhere to live. She had offered the place to young authors she liked, or to authors who had been recommended to her, and she was always very business-like about the terms of their stay.

She—aside from not charging them any rent—took care of the electricity and gas, did not (in theory; in practice she frequently did) take care of the telephone, and gave them money if they had none at all. They in return undertook to leave the apartment at the end of the year, or however long a period had been agreed upon; and to do some writing. (Only once had she had any trouble, and been forced to evict someone. It had been an unpleasant business; but necessary.) The fact that none of her tenants had fulfilled their promise had never worried her; she had never expected to see a prize rose bloom from every shoot she tended, and had always thought that if just one in her lifetime did, she would count herself lucky.

Yet as she lay in bed, going through these reasons for having maintained that apartment and all its inmates for so long, she found herself wondering if, deep down in her, she hadn't always known that those shoots wouldn't bloom, and, what was more, hadn't really wanted them to. She wondered, indeed, if far from trying to encourage imagination, she hadn't always been afraid of it, and had been hoping to keep it in check. Which was why she had always thought (though without malice) of her writers in residence as pets, and then lame dogs; and why, in another way, Gerhard's parting remark about David hadn't been so ridiculous. Perhaps her husband had always perceived, more clearly for once than herself, the motives for her so-called generosity; and perceived now that David Chezzel didn't, or wouldn't, meet her requirements. He wasn't, to return to the imagery of flowers, going to wither away; and he was, huge and scarlet, going to dominate her hitherto rose-less portion of the earth. He was going to overshadow her, he was going to draw all the goodness from the rest of her soil; and she, mere assistant gardener that she was, was going to find her life controlled by him. Controlled by the very fact of trying to keep *him* under control. . . .

No. Gerhard hadn't after all been so ridiculous. God knows why she *was* helping David to write this story. . . .

She turned over and told herself to stop being stupid. Being overshadowed. Being controlled. What nonsense. David was just a writer—a good one—who had, for the reason she had understood immediately, told her an unkind story. There was nothing more to it than that. She had no cause to be frightened —either of him, or his projected book—and she would not be. She supported him for exactly the same purpose as she had supported everyone else—which *was* to encourage him—and she was glad to do so. And now she would think about something else.

She would think, for example, about where Gerhard was. She would wonder if he was with Lucie Schmidt; and she would wonder, if he was, what they were talking about. . . .

In fact—there again because it would have required imagination to worry and wonder about such things, and she couldn't worry about the unknown—she fell asleep almost immediately; and it wasn't until the following morning, when she was having breakfast with Gerhard, that she really started to dwell on the subject of where her husband had been the night before. To dwell on it and, since he was sitting opposite her, to ask him.

'I think,' he said, 'I went out, had a few drinks, had dinner, had a few more drinks, then went to a movie somewhere.' He smiled across the table with his most disarming smile. 'But honestly I don't remember.'

Fran stared at him, trying to discover the truth in his eyes. She knew it was useless however. Gerhard's loss of memory when he had been drinking was one of the basic moves of his game; and she had never, throughout the fifteen years of their marriage, known whether he were bluffing. It happened on average once a month—though recently had been happening more often—and sometimes made her laugh, sometimes irritated her, sometimes made her admire him—if he were bluffing he bluffed with such a straight face it was impossible not to admire him—and sometimes, as this morning, made her very angry. It was too easy. Not to know anything—and by implication not to be responsible for anything—just because he had had a few drinks too many. Or to have a few drinks too many in order to say he didn't know anything, and wasn't responsible for anything.

For a moment she was tempted to challenge him; to tell him that he hadn't been drunk at all last night, knew perfectly well where he had been—with his French mistress—and had only used his dislike for modern music and the smell of cigarettes as an excuse to walk out on her. He had been intending to walk out anyway, and if she hadn't been smoking he would have found some other pretext for leaving. He would have told her that she was looking tired, or miserable, or old. . . . But partly because Cyrus too was sitting at the table, and she didn't like to reveal her anger to her son, and partly because she did know it was useless—he would blandly assure her that he had been bombed; and less blandly tell her that it was her own fault anyway; he really *couldn't* bear the smell of cigarettes, or the sound of that damn music she listened to— she held her tongue; and contented herself by remarking, sourly, that this was the third time in three weeks that he had been afflicted with amnesia, that if he weren't careful his condition would become chronic, and that it was very strange he was only so afflicted in the evenings. Why was it that however much he drank at lunch he always managed to retain his faculties throughout an afternoon at the office?

Now it was Gerhard's turn to seem about to lose his temper. His grey eyes gazed at her as if she were not just unattractive, but truly repulsive; and he pursed his lips as if he were about to spit. Then, like her—and probably, again, because of the boy—he managed to control himself. And smiling at her once more, he told her it was undoubtedly because though he did sometimes drink a lot at his business lunches, he never totally let himself go. Whereas as soon as he had finished work. . . .

'Anyway,' he added, as if the very idea were hilarious, 'where did you think I was? Out plotting with Lucie?'

That, Cyrus or no Cyrus, really would have made her explode—she would not have that woman's name mentioned in her house—if, even as she was trying, as it were, to take aim, to make sure the whole blast went off in that smug German face, her son himself hadn't defused her.

'Why,' he said brightly, 'doesn't Lucie stay with us any more when she's in New York?'

Because, Fran wanted to say, the last time she did I caught your father making love to her. Or if not that, and to be certain that Cyrus's sympathy was entirely with her: Because your father is planning to kill me and marry her. But naturally she said neither—the first was true, but might have upset the boy; the second, aside from upsetting him more, was definitely not true—and shrugged the question off with a murmured 'Because she prefers to stay in a hotel. She likes to be independent.' And by the time she had gathered her wits together to murmur this, the danger was over. Though if he ever *did* mention that name again, she told her husband with a glance, there would be such an explosion that the whole structure of their life together would come crashing down.

She had spent much of the evening before asking herself why she supported David Chezzel; she spent much of that day, after she had seen Cyrus off to school, had received a kind of apology from Gerhard—an apology that took the form of his asking her if it would be all right if he came to the ballet with her tonight —and had kissed him and wished him a good day at the office, asking herself why she supported her husband.

But though—as she spoke to friends on the phone, read the

paper, did some shopping, had lunch with her lawyer, went round a couple of galleries, met the editor of a literary magazine that she helped to finance, had tea with her mother, went home, talked and read a book with Cyrus, bathed and got ready for the ballet— she did ask herself this question, the answer she kept on giving herself was, at least superficially, far simpler than the answer she had given herself regarding David. She supported Gerhard because she loved him.

She had always believed that her looks, if they didn't precisely account for her intelligence, accounted for its nature. From the age of twelve or thirteen she had realized that she was not, nor was ever likely to be, a pretty girl. She had short thick legs, pudgy little hands, dull brown hair that was neither straight nor curly, and a face that had absolutely nothing special or striking about it. She had a small nose, a small mouth, and small eyes; that was all. To begin with she told herself she didn't care—her home life was very happy, and her quiet kind parents loved her as much as she loved them—and that she much preferred reading, listening to music, and going to the ballet, than dressing up and having boys ask her for dates. But inevitably perhaps, in a world so dominated by beautiful images, where appearance was held to be important, and an attractive appearance held to be desirable, her own less than beautiful image began, around the age of fourteen, to distress her. She could do, she instinctively realized, one of two things. The first was to flee from that distress, to feel upset, if not bitter about her looks, and to try to disguise them with carefully studied hair-styles, make-up, and clothes. The second was to face her distress head-on, analyse it, and attempt to see her longing for an attractive appearance for what she believed it was: either a longing to recapture the harmony of nature that she felt herself cut off from; or a longing to cut herself off entirely from nature, and make herself into a hard and brilliant artefact that was safe from the ravages of time, and the world. She chose, logically—since the first could only end in failure; in an ever more desperate flight, and bitterness—the second course. And having done so—having, that is, come to terms with her physical self—though she did, thereafter, have the occasional moment of regret that she didn't look like a movie-star or a ballet dancer, she never really worried about not being tall and slim and possessing huge dark eyes, and accepted that those boyfriends she did have would be attracted by her personality rather than by her face and figure.

She accepted and continued to believe this even when she realized that she was going, on her father's death—and indeed before—to be a very wealthy woman. Outside cheap novels, she couldn't imagine that anyone would be attracted to someone else for reasons other than personality or looks; the attraction of personality being obviously the preferable kind, and the only kind likely to provide a basis for a satisfactory relationship.

Such a lack, once again, of imagination, combined with an already well-developed intellectual arrogance (by the age of twenty she was firmly convinced that she could see through everyone's motives for all that they did; so that if there *were* such a creature in the real world as a man who cared only for money she would be able to spot him instantly), made her, clearly, vulnerable to attack. And when, at the age of twenty-nine, she *was* attacked—by a tall, blond, blue-eyed and athletic student of twenty-two, who had come to New York from his native Frankfurt in order, as he told her the first time they met, 'to seek his fortune'—she capitulated; without a struggle.

It was partly Gerhard's honesty that made her lay down her arms so willingly. (What he had told her was literally true.) It was partly his sense of fun; his brightness, his kindness, and the way he had of making her feel alive. ('Are you sure you're German?' she had asked him; for she too had her prejudices.) It was partly—despite her having risen above such things—his looks. But above all, it was his ability, as she saw it, to stay in the world—not being sheltered, as she was, by her family, her wealth, and the small closed circle of friends in which she lived—and to be uncorrupted by it. It was all very well for her to be, as she sincerely tried to be, good and aware and on the side of life. The house she had been born into had been built on stilts; and she had been able to gather her strength up there, in comparative safety, before setting out to explore—still from the comparative safety of a car that had been armoured by culture and security and money—the jungle. But for Gerhard to be, as she sincerely believed he was, good and aware and on the side of life, was altogether more of an achievement. For he, on the contrary, had been born in the jungle itself. He had been raised by parents who were, according to him, drunken, ignorant, and brutal; and had had, though he called himself a student, little formal education. To have survived at all under such circumstances struck Fran as being wonderful; to have survived as well as he had—still to prefer the sun to the cold dead moon—seemed positively miraculous.

She had her doubts, naturally. He was, compared to her, a mere child. He tended, at times, to drink too much. He didn't care for any of the things she cared for. (Though he said he was quite prepared to care for them.) She didn't care, she claimed, for the one thing he claimed to care for: cash. He didn't have, as she hoped she had, and thought everyone should have, any—as she perhaps priggishly termed it—sense of living in a society. (He believed in looking after himself, and all that, or only that, which was necessary to his well-being. He also believed that everyone else should do the same. Any other course of action was, he claimed, mere self-deception and falsity. And self-deception and falsity could only lead to personal unhappiness, and general misery.) And she knew he would never really be a friend of her friends; though he would always be good-natured and pleasant with them, and was too smart to—or anyway smart enough not to—feel threatened by them.

But when he told her that he loved her and asked her to marry him; and told her further that if she accepted him she would never have reason to regret it—if the contract was, to put it crudely, his love in exchange for her money (with her own love thrown in as an extra), he would keep his side of the bargain if she kept hers—she cast her doubts aside. And having received the blessing of her parents, who told her that in spite of everything they couldn't help liking Gerhard, and the approval of nearly all her friends—who told her, loathe though many were to say it, the same—Fran left the Englishman she had been involved with for the previous five years, and had vaguely assumed she would one day marry—he was very tall, very thin, and was a musicologist whose special field was modern Eastern European music—exchanged the small apartment in Greenwich Village she had been living in for a penthouse on Park Avenue, and told the young German yes.

Gerhard was right. She never did have reason to regret it. Her husband was nearly everything she had hoped he would be. (And if it hadn't been for his occasional drinking bouts, and consequent amnesia, he would have been absolutely everything.) He had been bright and fun and kind before the marriage; he became more so as the years passed. He had made her feel alive when she had met him; with time, he not only made her feel alive, but even—she who had always thought of herself as having been born old—young. Her parents and friends who, while giving her their blessing, had had some misgivings about the match, were, ten years after the wedding, almost more charmed with her mate than she was. He was immensely generous with anyone he liked—and he liked practically everyone—and he was able to talk to and get on with the oddest assortment of people; people who Fran herself couldn't talk to, or get on with. Often, at parties, Gerhard could be seen sitting quietly in a corner chatting with the most notoriously reticent writer, smiling about something with the most violently rich-hating socialist, or making fun of, and laughing with, the most extreme feminists.

At times Fran was tempted to subscribe to his philosophy of total selfishness. . . .

In fact, until a few years ago, the union couldn't have been happier, or more successful. But then, one spring, they had gone to Paris together on business. While there, they had had dinner in a restaurant with some French colleagues of Gerhard's. And amongst these colleagues had been Lucie Schmidt.

Fran, later, hated to admit it; but it was she, in the first instance, who had become friendly with the woman. She supposed the reason was that Lucie, in a way, and aside from being in the same business, was a female version of Gerhard. (Which was also the reason, probably, why Gerhard, to begin with, took one of his rare dislikes to her.) She was the same age as Fran, and she couldn't have been described as beautiful. Her nose was too big, her chin was too small, and her hair was too untidy. Yet in spite of this, in spite of a tiresome habit of being endlessly foul-mouthed in four different languages, and in spite of an even more tiresome habit of turning every conversation round to sex, she was immensely attractive. Because she had a beautiful body—above all beautiful legs—because she made clothes, that on anyone else would have looked drab, look wonderful, and because, notwithstanding her continuous swearing and her obsession with sex, she was fun, and alive, very bright—and no fool. (Fran got the impression that the swearing and the talk about sex were put out as a smoke-screen in order to hide this last fact *from* fools. Especially from fools with intellectual pretensions.) What was more, not only did she like Lucie, but Lucie liked her. For the first five minutes in the restaurant the Frenchwoman tried to shock the American. But after that—having apparently failed—she relaxed; and the two of them got on as well together as friends who had known each other for years.

A month later Lucie came to New York, and phoned Fran; who invited her to lunch, and went with her to the ballet. ('Don't ask me,' Gerhard said. 'I find it hard enough to enjoy ballet at the best of times. If I had to sit next to that spoiled little bitch I'd probably go mad.')

Four months later, when Lucie came again to New York (partly for business, and partly to see an ex-husband she was fond of), she stayed, at Fran's insistence, and against Gerhard's wishes, at the penthouse on Park Avenue.

Three months later, she came again.

And it was on the seventh day of this second stay, one evening when Cyrus had gone to Connecticut with his grandparents, during a party in honour of some visiting South American novelist, that Fran, almost by accident (she hadn't noticed that they were missing, and had gone to Lucie's room to fetch something), found her husband making love with her guest.

She would have assumed, if she'd ever thought about it, that she would behave with perfect calm in such a situation. But maybe because she hadn't ever thought about it, she did something which shocked her more than the actual discovery. She lost her head, and had hysterics. She started screaming. She rushed over to the bed and started punching and pummelling the naked bodies lying there, wanting to tear out those eyes that were staring at her. (Gerhard staring with fear; Lucie with delighted triumph.) She spat, she pushed, she cried, she scratched. She fought off Gerhard's attempts to hold her, and she shrieked 'I don't give a damn,' when he told her that all her guests must be listening to her. (Whether they were or not she never knew, but she doubted it; Lucie's room was a long way from the living room, and everyone there was making a great deal of noise.) And finally she ordered Lucie out of the house. 'Now, this minute. If you're not gone in five minutes I'll kill you.'

Later that night Gerhard told her that Lucie had been trying to get him into bed ever since she'd arrived; that her hysteria had been unnecessary and ridiculous—'I never could stand her and I still can't; I was just drunk and if you hadn't found us I would have forgotten I'd done it tomorrow'—and that in any case Fran's insistence that Lucie stay with them had been a kind of challenge to him. She had so pointedly ignored his own views on the subject that he had felt she was testing him. And he didn't like or approve of tests.

He had done, he shouted, no more than she had wanted him to do. . . .

Which might, Fran told herself a few days after, be true. Or at least have an element of truth in it. Which in turn—together with the fact that she had exposed, with her reaction, a corner of her character she hadn't known existed, couldn't, for all her much-vaunted self-knowledge, account for, and was, in any case, bitterly ashamed of (to behave like that just because two people are making love!)—would explain why she wasn't able to forgive Lucie Schmidt or Gerhard (or, if it came to it, herself), and why she had forbidden Gerhard ever to see 'that whore' again. Forbidden him despite her realization that by so doing she was ensuring he would. For Gerhard didn't like being forbidden to do things any more than he liked being tested.

How often he saw her she didn't know, though she did her best to find out; even contemplating having an investigator follow him. It wasn't very often, she suspected—Lucie was based in Paris—but it was often enough for the wound to be kept open, and aching; and for her hatred of the woman to become an obsession. She would dream of Lucie Schmidt; she would spend hours willing Lucie Schmidt to be killed in a car crash, or a plane crash, or to have something fall on her head as she walked by a construction site; and she would spend longer hours discussing first with friends, and then with anyone who would listen, how she could prevent her husband from seeing Lucie Schmidt again.

Which made, of course, matters worse. For not only did nothing that was said help her, but the very parading round town of the affair enraged Gerhard; and made him all the more determined to continue it.

(Some people told Fran she should be calm, forget the whole business, and stop making a mountain out of a mole-hill. Others told her she should see a psychiatrist, who would help her to come to terms with her rage. And others still told her she should leave, or threaten to leave, Gerhard. All of which advice was worthless because 'the business' *was* a mountain; because she had always been proud of her ability to come to terms with herself by herself, and she didn't want to lose her pride, which was her ultimate defence against all the possible hurts of this world; and because—this above all—she had no real reason to leave Gerhard.)

Finally, however, and perhaps inevitably, time came to her assistance. Her husband was having an intermittent relationship with a Frenchwoman. It was as simple as that. She didn't like it, but couldn't do a thing about it; and after it had been going on for two years she no longer had the energy to dwell constantly on the wretched fact. Her obsession didn't vanish; but she did manage to put it into storage, and keep it mainly out of sight.

And out of sight it had remained, more or less, until three months ago. Until, that is, Fran had noticed—and remarked upon the fact—that Gerhard was drinking more than normal; and until she had heard first, through friends of friends, that Lucie Schmidt was back in town, and then that she was planning to stay for a while.

Yet though, when she did hear it, her obsession once more

loomed up before her, at least this time Fran was able to prevent its shadow from falling on her face; and at least this time, apart from a couple of fights with Gerhard (both occasioned by her not finding him at the office when she had phoned him there) she didn't allow it to interfere with her daily life too much. Three years ago she had been forever cancelling parties and dinners and meetings. . . . What was more, since she not only still loved her husband, but also still didn't regret having married him—which, she reflected now, as she finished dressing for the ballet, was another reason why she continued to support him—she tried not to push him further into a corner, and stopped herself from going around telling everyone of this latest development. In fact she only told one person.

That person was David Chezzel.

Partly because she realized she had a share of the blame, Fran hardly thought, over the next few weeks, of the book that David claimed to be writing. Though she did have other reasons as well. One was that the story the man had outlined was not of a kind that interested her; she was not a fan of the murder mystery, whatever form it took. And another was that Gerhard, from the evening of the ballet onwards, had become so attentive and kind to her, seemed so eager to apologize for the wrongs he had done her over the last four years, and was so willing to do whatever she wanted—unprecedently he accompanied her to London for a week, to attend a poetry festival—that she began to hope that Lucie Schmidt was a thing of the past. Indeed, her husband was with her so much of the time—he almost stopped drinking, never phoned to say he was going to be tied up, and didn't have a single attack of amnesia—that she didn't see when, even if he'd wanted to, he could have met his French mistress.

(She made herself stop calling him at the office; and after

she had stopped, he started to call her. Sometimes twice a day. . . .)

And probably she wouldn't have thought again about that book—at any rate not until it was finished, and she read it; but then she would have been able to think about it, and judge it, on purely literary grounds—if, two months after she had been told the story, she hadn't, very faintly at first, and then more persistently—started to suffer from pains in the stomach.

Even so it took her almost a week to admit to herself that she was thinking about it; and to admit that she was wondering whether Gerhard was poisoning her. . . .

She had never, she thought, as she left her doctor—he couldn't discover what was wrong—been so angry with herself in her life. Here she was, Fran Niebauer, suspecting her husband of trying to murder her. It was pitiful. I am a forty-six-year-old woman living in New York City, she told herself, who is fortunate enough to have a wonderful son, a husband whom she loves, a great many friends, abundant money, and a life that is interesting and enjoyable. And I am wondering whether I am being poisoned! It was preposterous; and she had been right, she added, to despise murder mysteries. Oh sure—it was perfectly possible that she would be killed in an accident, or might suddenly have a stroke or develop cancer—it was even possible that she would be attacked by a madman in the street. These things she was prepared to accept as the normal risks of day to day living. But she was not prepared to accept the idea that her husband, whatever he thought of her, was tipping little powders into her food, or into her wine, or—or—she didn't know. She *didn't* have any imagination, and she was thankful for it. All she did know was that she was a civilized human being, married to another civilized human being, and that as far as she was concerned civilized human beings did not go round killing one another. If Gerhard wanted to leave her he would, once he had taken his decision, tell her, and then proceed to do so. She would be upset naturally—more than upset; she would be bitterly unhappy—but she would accommodate her unhappiness just as she had accommodated her unattractiveness, and she would go on living. She did love her husband, and she hoped he would always be with her—but he was not the be all and end all of her life. Apart from anything else, she thought—staring the absurdity in the face— he had no reason to wish her dead. All right, she did support him in a life-style he couldn't have afforded without her; but on the other hand he also earned plenty himself, in the fashion importing business she had set him up in. He could have lived on that, even with Lucie Schmidt, in more than adequate comfort.

And really to clinch the matter, even if, for some inconceivable reason, Gerhard did want to kill her, he could hardly have done so now; not after she had told him the story of David Chezzel's book. Because not only would she know what he was doing, but, when the book was published, the whole world would know what he had done. After all, it would be pretty obvious. . . .

She was so angry with herself that instead of walking home from the doctor's, as she would normally have done on such a warm, sunny April morning, she took a taxi. And then, which was still less normal, as she was paying the driver, she changed her mind; and told the man that she wanted to go to the West Side. She gave him David's address.

She never called on people unannounced; it wasn't fair, or civilized. She also had never disturbed any of her writers in residence—not even with a phone-call—during the day; or during the night, if they told her that that was when they worked. Today however was an exceptional day; and since David had so disturbed her, she felt she had an excuse for her behaviour. What she was going to say when she saw him—if he were in, and if he answered the door—she wasn't sure of. All she was sure of was that she wanted to speak to him; and, possibly, to see if he wouldn't replace the genie that he was in the process of conjuring up back into its bottle. Or to see, if he himself were the genie, whether she couldn't in some way persuade him to return to captivity.

Once again—and it came to her with another attack of her stomach cramps—the idea of threatening the writer with eviction entered her head. Once again, and for the same reasons as before, she rejected it. But she did so with less conviction than before. After all, she thought, if—But then she stopped. There were no ifs. She was *not* being poisoned. And she was being incredibly stupid. . . .

She didn't, however, change her mind a second time as regards her destination.

David was in; and he answered the door. He also assured her he wasn't working—he had done his four hours for the day—and offered her a drink. Which she accepted.

When she was sitting, glass in hand, looking at the author, she realized he was looking at her; wanting an explanation for her visit.

She had thought, coming up in the elevator, that she would start by being perfectly straightforward; telling David that she had been hurt by the story he had told, and now, absurdly, had got the notion that Gerhard was trying to poison her. And she was about to do it. But all at once she hesitated. Which made her feel more angry with herself than ever. For God's sake, she ordered herself, say what you have to say. But whether because she was suddenly too ashamed to reveal her stupidity, or whether because she suddenly felt that certain things were better not talked about, she couldn't, when it came to it, do it.

Instead she looked around the high-ceilinged, red-carpeted, well-proportioned living room, and murmured that David had made it look very nice, with the paintings he had put on the walls, and the plants he had placed all around. (She provided the furniture, and paid for the apartment to be painted every other year; decorations of whatever sort, and—as in this case— plants, she left to the discretion of her tenants.)

Then she went on to remark that David himself was looking well. (Which she supposed he was; though to be honest she found his looks unpleasant. He wasn't very tall, and while his face wasn't ugly, there was something distasteful about it. His brown eyes were a little too sincere and frank. His thick black hair was a little too glossy. And his lips were a little too eager to break into a self-deprecating smile. He ranked, in fact, in her canine terminology, as a lap-dog; and lap-dogs disgusted her.

Which made it all the more ironic that he should promise to be her first champion; whereas all those other rangy, fierce, spirited young things had turned out to be creatures of little or no worth; with empty barks, an unoriginal and undistinguished way of holding themselves, and no staying power.)

Finally she said that she had been passing, had realized that it was quite a time since she had seen him—which was true; she hadn't wanted to, and hadn't invited him to any of her parties over the last two months—and had thought she would drop by to make sure everything was all right. No problems with the plumbing, with the neighbours, or anything like that. . . .

But then, since there were really no more topics available to her, and since David was still watching her, waiting for her to say what she had come to say, she could put it off no longer. And telling herself that it didn't matter how foolish she sounded, and how even the unspeakable at times had to be spoken—she plunged.

She delivered the speech she had prepared in the elevator; and David listened to her in silence. When she had finished he told her, as he had on the phone, and with the same self-righteous indignation, that she was being paranoid. This time, however, there was no laugh afterwards.

'For heaven's sake, Fran,' he said, 'it's just a book. Just a story.'

He was small; but she was smaller. And he was looking down on her.

'Maybe your telling me about Gerhard and his French-woman gave me the idea, but how I develop that idea is nothing to do with Gerhard or you or any Frenchwoman. It's to do with me. It sounds as if your pains are psychosomatic.'

Fran wasn't sure if she believed in psychosomatic pains; at least not for herself. If she did, she certainly didn't approve of them.

'David, I'm not an idiot. You know that.'

The brown eyes were wide now; the mouth severe.

'Yes, Fran, I do know that. Which is why I don't really understand what you're talking about. Do you think that Gerhard and I worked all this out together?'

'No, of course not. I just thought—' she shrugged. 'Maybe, after I told Gerhard the story, he decided it was quite a good one.' She shook her head. 'No. That's not true. I don't believe it for a minute. And you're right not to understand me. I'm being ridiculous. I guess I'm upset because Lucie is in New York, and presumably Gerhard is seeing her occasionally. That's probably why I've got these cramps.'

David relaxed slightly, and did allow himself a smile now. It was condescending.

'Gerhard's not about to leave you,' he murmured. 'Apart from your cash, I'm sure he likes you.'

Fran would have liked to smile too. She couldn't.

'Yes, I think he does. What I don't understand is what *she* gets out of it. Just sex?'

'I don't know. I've never met her.'

'What about in the book. What are the motives of the "other woman" in that?'

David paused, and Fran thought he wasn't going to answer. But eventually, with a frown of irritation, he did.

'She is a bored woman who doesn't have enough brains to see why she's bored, or enough energy to seek a genuine remedy for her boredom. So she travels as much as she can, and has the occasional affair, and persuades herself she is having fun. She isn't really, she knows she isn't, but—the married man in New York she is going with does, essentially, just represent sex to her. Or a little adventure. Something to do when she is in New York. She has no intention of getting seriously involved with him. *He* even bores her slightly. Until, that is, he proposes killing his wife. Then he becomes more interesting. The adventure promises to be more fun than she'd imagined. Of course she doesn't want to have anything to do with the actual murder—she doesn't like trouble—any more than she wants to marry the man if the plot succeeds. Once the deed is done the fun will be over; and she isn't interested in the money the man will get from his wife. Though he of course doesn't realize this.'

Fran remembered Lucie saying, 'I don't give a damn about money. I was born poor and I'll die poor. In between I'll get by as best I can.'

'Does,' she asked David, 'the woman work?'

'Yes, I think so. But I'm not sure yet. I'm not really very far into the book. And I've hardly touched on the character of the Frenchwoman. I've been concentrating on the wife so far.'

'Does she know she's going to be killed?'

'She suspects. But—' David smiled again. 'In that respect she's like you. She refuses to believe her own suspicions. She tells herself it's ridiculous. That "civilized" people don't kill each other.'

'They don't,' Fran said sharply.

'Oh Fran dear, do stop it. Of course they don't.'

Fran wondered. . . .

'And what happens in the end?'

'There again I'm not certain yet. Maybe the husband does it, and gets the money, or maybe—he doesn't. I don't know.'

'Why,' Fran asked finally, 'doesn't the wife change her will, leave her money to someone else, when she starts to suspect what is happening?'

'Because that would be an admission that she *does* believe it is happening. And being a convinced rationalist, she cannot bring herself to make this admission. She would rather die than allow the irrational to enter her world. Indeed she would die if she did, because her entire life is built upon the premise that one must deny the irrational, and without this premise she couldn't go on.'

Fran nodded. She looked out of the window. She remembered that she was taking Cyrus to Hunter College this afternoon, to see a children's show. She remembered she had an English publisher and his wife coming for drinks at six. She remembered that she had to finish reading two books; and that Gerhard had promised to drive her to Princeton tomorrow, to see a young woman they had recently met who wrote short stories.

She remembered that she was a woman who lived in a small body in a small world, and had always, more or less, controlled both.

She stood up and said 'David, I know I *am* being ridiculous, and that my pains probably are imaginary, and that I have no right to ask you this. But will you please do me a favour and not write any more of your book.'

There was no hint of apology in her voice; no trace of weakness. She wanted something; and she had asked for it.

For a while then there was silence. David looked at his

hands. He looked round the room—round *her* room—and up at the ceiling. He looked at her, and made her feel that while she had never been more unattractive in her life, she had never cared less. He looked back at his hands. And only after perhaps half a minute did he speak.

'No,' he said, with a directness that equalled, briefly, her own. 'No, I'm sorry.'

Then his directness collapsed. The eyes shone with sincerity. The generally smooth forehead crumpled with concern. The lips were about to utter some self-condemnation. He came over to her and put his arms around her. He kissed her cheek. He said 'Oh Fran, I wish I could. Honestly. I know how upsetting all this must be for you. But you don't really mean it. You don't really want me to give it up. You just think you do. But really, my dear, I can't. It's—' he gave a soft laugh—'it's as if you were asking me to have an abortion. And I can't.' He paused. 'Why don't you and Gerhard take a vacation? Go to Europe. Go to Mexico. Go anywhere. I'm sure your pains would stop then. Gerhard does love you, you know that. And I love you. Everyone loves you. Really. You're wonderful. So don't be silly now. Please.'

He could fawn all he liked. He could go down on his knees in front of her. His eyes could fill with tears. But he was, now, stronger than her, and he knew it; and she knew he was not about to renounce his strength. She stood there, stiff between his arms, and told herself that she despised him. She told herself she should say 'in that case I must ask you to quit this apartment.' (Though she knew even now that she wouldn't.) She told herself that since she had nothing more to say she should leave. She wanted to go home.

Still though, for a while, she didn't move; and still she searched for a solution. What if, she thought, she bribed the man. Surely if she offered him enough he would renounce his precious baby. Or perhaps she should threaten to write to his publishers and warn them that if they took the book she would sue them. Or perhaps. . . .

But it was all useless. She suspected she had no grounds on which to sue. If there were grounds she realized that if she couldn't bring herself to threaten him with eviction, she certainly couldn't bring herself to take that step. And she was sure that however much money she did offer him he would still refuse; if only because his hatred was as necessary to him as her sense of reason was to her. And that it was hatred that inspired David, she suddenly became positive. . . .

She released herself from his embrace, and shook her head. 'Let's smoke a cigarette together,' she said, 'and then I must go.'

'Yes,' David murmured; and then 'You *do* understand, don't you, Fran?'

Yes, she did, Fran told herself ten minutes later, out once more in the street. It was as she had perceived when she had first heard the story, and as she had further perceived a little while ago. David did not like to feel dependent on her. Because he was dependent on her, he hated her and everything she stood for. And out of his hatred he created. . . .

(She wondered if, when he became successful, he would lose his hatred. Probably not, she thought. It would even grow. For then he would be more than ever dependent. On critics. On publishers. On the book-buying public. On all those people who held the ropes which kept him suspended up there in the spotlight. Of course he would reason that it was him, on his intellectual trapeze, that the crowds were watching. And he would be right. Nevertheless, he would resent the fact that he was performing in someone else's circus; a circus of whose management he did not necessarily approve, and to whose profits and maintenance he was contributing.)

Yet though she told herself all this, and was sure that she had understood David's motives for writing his book, Fran couldn't help feeling, in that warm spring morning, not so much angry now at her absurdity, as, once again, frightened. Because having failed to get the genie back into its bottle, she sensed that for the first time in her adult life she was starting to lose that control she had always had. It was horrifying; to have the sidewalk beneath her feet shake and sway and crack. . . . Especially when she knew the composition of the stones; knew who had laid them, who maintained them, what was beneath them. And more especially when, in spite of all her knowledge, she was certain that if she did lose her balance, if she were to slip through one of those cracks, she would be plunged into chaos; into a world where nothing was solid, nothing was real, and nothing at all could be controlled. It was so horrifying that for a moment she was on the point of abandoning herself altogether, and bursting into tears; or of racing back to David and forcing him to give up his book, whatever means she had to employ. But it was only for a moment. Then she pulled herself together, and forced herself to think of something else. To think again, for example, since indignation was still the dominant emotion within her, of David's character; and more particularly, of what David himself had told her about that character, one evening several months ago.

He had been born, he said, in Texas. His father was a mild ineffectual man who had been semi-crippled by a fall from a ladder, and who stayed home after his accident and invented things. His mother was a brisk, practical, over-bearing woman who owned a store and kept the large family going. He was the fourth of seven children. Superficially, they had all gotten on well together, but deeper down his brothers and sisters had distrusted him. Not because he considered himself superior to them intellectually—though he guessed he did—but because of something soft, sly, underhand in his manner. He was always friendly, ingratiating, ready to go along, in family discussions,

with his mother's idea or opinions. But the second her back
was turned—he struck. He would scratch her. He would claw
her. He would tear her to pieces. He was like a cat, his brothers
and sisters told him; and he looked like a cat. Smooth and
sleek and impeccably groomed. Yet in spite of this distrust,
he never felt lonely. Because he adored his lame irresponsible
father; and because though he didn't like his mother, and the
way she ruled the household, and though he did attempt to
destroy her in the eyes of the other children, he never allowed
her to see what he felt, and what he did. Nor, he was convinced,
did she.

'That way,' he had told Fran, 'I felt safe. On the one hand
I had the company of someone who made me laugh, who made
me feel cheerful, and who interested me—and on the other I
had the protection of the person who ran the show. Which I
guess,' he had added, 'has been the story of my life ever since.
Only I've generalized it over the years, and while my possibly
sentimental love of the happy and unreflecting has grown, my
hatred of the rulers has also grown. But I still spend most of
my time with one or other of the two groups. Either with the
gypsies, or with the tyrants.

'I started writing, I guess, when I finally did pluck up the
courage to denounce the tyrants. To denounce them for the
violence and the cruelty, the selfishness and the greed that lies
behind their often reasonable and civilized exteriors. That lies
behind their professions of acting for the general good. But do
you know something? Either their blindness, their stupidity,
or their sense of guilt is such that they've never noticed what
I'm doing. Or my slyness is such that I've managed to disguise
my voice, so they don't really hear what I'm saying.'

Until now, Fran thought, as she turned east, deciding to
walk home across the park. Until now. . . .

She couldn't help admitting, however, as her fear returned
with renewed force, that she herself, until this morning, had

been stupid and blind. She should have realized, six months ago when David had told her that tale, that in spite of his repeated claims to love her, he included her among the rulers he loathed. As indeed she should have realized to what extent it *was* this loathing that inspired him. . . .

Stupid and blind she may have been. Nevertheless, just as before Fran had not allowed herself to think of David's novel, so, over the following weeks, she did not—could not—allow herself to be overcome by her fear. Her fear that Gerhard, having heard of that novel, was now following its plot; chapter by chapter. . . . She *had*, she told herself as her pains grew steadily worse, to be calm; and she had to seek the rational explanation.

She went, accordingly, to several different doctors; and when she had heard from all of them that they didn't know what was wrong, she contemplated swallowing her pride, and going to consult a psychiatrist.

Before taking such a step, however, she thought it only right that she discuss the matter with Gerhard. Which she did one evening in the middle of May.

They were sitting in their living room, and she started by saying that recently—since her pains had started, come to think of it—she had begun to dislike this room. For years, with its comfortable sofas, its beautiful old English furniture, its mainly modern paintings, it had seemed to her one of the pleasantest of rooms. Now though—something had happened to it. It looked, she complained, stiff and awkward. Unnatural. She felt as if she were sitting in a stage-set.

'Nonsense,' Gerhard, sprawled out on one of the sofas with a glass of wine in his hand, told her. 'It's because you're not feeling well. Everyone feels like that when they're sick.'

'Talking of sickness,' Fran said, smiling at her husband—

who had been more kind and attentive than ever of late—'I think I'm going to go to an analyst next week.'

Gerhard, who had always disliked analysis as much as she had, though for different reasons—whereas she believed that she was strong enough to master herself, he wasn't remotely interested in mastering himself—frowned. 'What kind of analyst?'

'A psychoanalyst. A psychiatrist.'

'What in God's name for? You don't think you're imagining your pains, do you?'

'No, of course I'm not imagining them. But what I am imagining may be the cause of those pains. Or what I'm imagining may be a symptom of my sickness.'

Gerhard smiled at her now; his way of telling her to go on, and explain herself.

'You mustn't be mad with me. But you see since David told me the story of that book, and since I did start getting these cramps, in the back of my mind I have the idea that you're poisoning me.'

She had expected Gerhard either to be amused, or, despite her telling him he mustn't, to be angry.

And since he normally behaved as was expected, she was relieved when he was both.

He began by laughing—narrowing his eyes and saying 'Oh Fran'—and then, seeing that she was serious, went on to become indignant, and slightly sulky.

'Jesus,' he pouted. 'That's charming.'

Fran, sitting in a straight-backed chair, shrugged.

'There's no point in being coy about it. That is what I've been thinking. And that's why I think I should see a psychiatrist.'

'Yes.' Gerhard hesitated. 'I guess you should.'

There was silence for a while; then Fran asked the question she couldn't help asking.

'You're *not* poisoning me, are you?'

Now she expected him really to flare up; even to storm out of the house and come back tomorrow suffering from amnesia.

But this time Gerhard did not do what was expected of him. Which made his wife feel first disconcerted, and then truly alarmed.

He sat up on the sofa; he stared at her with the expression of a hurt child; and he murmured, with a helpless little gesture of the hands, 'Even if I were I'd obviously deny it, wouldn't I? So—no, I'm not.'

Fran stared back at him. It wasn't so much what he had said that alarmed her, as the way he had said it; as that helpless little gesture. He suddenly looked to her like a person sitting on a stage, playing a part that he wasn't happy with, yet which he couldn't not play. Either because he didn't have the strength of will to defy the author, who had written the part just for him; or because he realized that if he didn't accept this role, there would be no other for him. And he couldn't live without acting. . . .

Just as she, she thought, so small and dumpy, so rich and unattractive, was like an actress who had been cast in the role of the victim.

Or perhaps, more than being like actors and actresses on a stage, they were like characters in a story. Sitting in a room that had been described as having comfortable sofas, beautiful old English furniture, and mainly modern paintings. . . .

Outside, and far below, she could hear the sound of traffic; and the sirens of police cars, racing to the scene of a crime.

In her fear, Fran did at last force herself to smile. But her voice, when she spoke, was sharp.

'In any case,' she said, as she had said to herself before, 'you have no reason to wish me dead, have you? After all, we're happy together, and if we weren't, you'd leave me.' She added: 'Wouldn't you?'

'Yes, of course.' Gerhard stood up, came over to her, and held out his hands. 'And now let's go to bed.'

Fran smiled again, and let herself be virtually lifted to her feet. As she let herself be led to the bedroom, undressed, and, as yet another attack of her pains hit her, put to bed.

And it wasn't until she was in bed, wincing and clutching her husband's hand, that Gerhard, softly, concluded their conversation.

Stroking, with his free hand, her forehead, he murmured: 'But you know one thing, Fran. You'd never let me go even if I wanted to. I mean you probably couldn't stop me actually going, but you'd destroy me once I had gone. Destroy the business. Destroy everything. I mean—not only make sure I didn't have a cent, but make sure I didn't even have a pillow to rest my head on.' It was his turn then to add: 'Wouldn't you?'

But Fran didn't reply. And biting her lips, she simply clung to her husband, thought that he was probably right—she wouldn't allow this most precious of all her possessions to slip from her grasp—and told herself miserably that maybe, if there were any truth in this absurd tale, she had got things the wrong way round. Till now, when entertaining the ridiculous notion that she was being poisoned, she had believed that David had given Gerhard the idea of killing her. But what if Gerhard had already made his plans, David had somehow discovered, or guessed what he was doing, and had seen in the plot the material for a good book; for the good book that Fran Niebauer had always hoped he would write. . . .

If David had told her directly what was happening—or even given her proof—Gerhard would have changed his mind, and the story would have fizzled out. Loathing her as he did, David didn't want Gerhard to change his mind. So telling her by way of the book he had both warned her, and salved his conscience, and also, since he knew that she would never believe him, had assured Gerhard that he could go ahead and do what he wanted, without any interference. Just as long as he, David Chezzel, had the exclusive rights. (And he would of course, Fran saw now, change the characters and the situation enough so that no one would recognize the people or the event on which they were based.)

It wasn't, in that case, a matter of life imitating art—a concept Fran had never had much patience with—but, as usual, just a matter of art imitating life. And it was, she told herself, perfect. Or it would have been if it *were* true.

Which it wasn't. It wasn't. She simply had some so far unexplained pains in her stomach. Really.

She spent much of that night lying awake telling herself this, and thinking, once again, of Gerhard. Of the Gerhard whom she loved. Of the Gerhard whom she controlled. . . .

Towards dawn she asked herself if she did want to control her world, and everyone in it, because the world outside was appalling, and she wanted to be safe from it; or if she wanted that control because she *feared* that the world outside was appalling. She would have liked to think it was the former— and considering the evidence of history she was more than justified in doing so—but she was afraid it was in fact the latter. It was *fear* that had made her retire into her book-lined, record-filled penthouse. And not even fear of the known—of the horrors that history revealed—but fear of the unknown. Of the imaginary. For the known, however terrible, could be accommodated. Whereas the unknown. . . .

But what choice did she have, she cried to herself as she decided to get up and make herself some tea. She hadn't chosen her refuge; she had, by the circumstances of her birth, been forced into it. Just as Gerhard, by the circumstances of his birth had been forced into *his* refuge; into building up ramparts of houses and cars and silk suits and bank accounts. Just as everyone, in one way or another, was forced into some refuge. Some people made their walls of religion; some of art. Some of sex; some of power. Some—many—of money; some of reason. But while they were all more or less safe within their ramparts—safe from the monstrous, mythical creatures who wandered round outside—if something, something at times as apparently inconsequential as a stomach-ache, were to slip through a crack in those bricks—oh, then everything started to tumble. In her case it *had* been a stomach-ache. In Gerhard's case it had possibly been something equally as trivial; something that had suddenly brought infection into his isolated ward, and caused him, in his panic, to attempt to seal over the cracks. To prop up the toppling walls with affairs, and dreams of murder. . . .

No. No! It wasn't so. Gerhard was not dreaming of murder. His word had *not* become infected. It was only her's that had been; and she *would* keep up her barricade of reason. She had to. . . .

She did; but within another month she had been obliged to retrench and retrench, until there was almost nothing left in her world apart from the word 'reason'. And now more than feeling that a germ had entered her, she came to feel that she had allowed a guest into the hallway of her house; a guest who had started to consume everything in sight. The pictures and the furniture had gone first; then the floors and ceilings; and finally her husband, her parents, her belief in and love of literature, and her belief and faith in civilization. In fact virtually all that remained at this stage was a tattered carpet on which she was flying through space; with the intruder tearing at its border, snapping and chewing at its edges.

But still, as she lay in bed all day, wracked continually by her pains, almost unable to eat, she fought it off. Still she told herself, as she saw doctors and psychiatrists (who could agree on nothing but that she was seriously ill), and as she submitted to further tests, she would not give in. She was not being poisoned. She was *not*. For if she were she would have at last to look her guest directly in the face. And still she couldn't bear that prospect. The prospect of seeing the face of hatred, madness and death. . . .

Yet—she hadn't, even now, been entirely abandoned. She did, even now, have some outside help. And determined though she was to cling to her rug of reason, she knew that without this steadying hand she wouldn't have been able to manage it. She would, sooner or later, have slipped.

This one remaining person, this only surviving companion of her flight, was, perhaps inevitably, her son, Cyrus; and the help he gave her was simply to remind her, or make her aware, that he was also the one person she did not control; and never had. (Of course she had never controlled Lucie Schmidt, who was in a way the source of all her problems. But that was neither here nor there. Because apart from the first few months of their acquaintance Lucie had never been in her world—she had indeed been firmly barred from it—and she didn't pretend to control those who were not hers to control.) Why she didn't control Cyrus—and why, looking back, her parents had never controlled her—and why he rather controlled her, was because she loved him. Naturally she loved her mother and father, and Gerhard too; but that was a conditional love. (The condition being that they played their parts as parents and husband, and did not, so to speak, branch out on their own, and force her to rearrange her own character in order to accommodate theirs.) Whereas the love she had for Cyrus was unconditional; and though many of her friends told her she was wrong, she would have been prepared, if it had come to it, to sacrifice herself for her son; which she would not have been prepared to do for anyone else. She hoped it would never come to it, and saw no reason why it should; sacrifices in her opinion tended to breed devils, not appease them. Nevertheless, in the final analysis—in an 'only room for one person at the top of the tower' situation—she would have done it.

Her son, to her, was wonderful. He was wonderful because he seemed everything a child should be—joyful and interested, not especially good, and not especially bad. He was wonderful because if she had always thought of herself as spirit, and Gerhard as flesh, she saw Cyrus as a synthesis of both. He was wonderful because when he was good he was good without affectation; and when he was bad he was bad without being evil. He was wonderful because he didn't, as yet, appear to take refuge behind any ramparts or walls. And he was wonderful above all because though he did control her, and was, presumably, if only unconsciously, aware of doing so, he in no way threatened to destroy her. (As, she was convinced, anyone else would have done if she had allowed them power over her.) He was like a piece of music to which she could open herself so completely that its melody and harmonies filled every inch of her; yet a piece of music which, far from diminishing her, made her feel more complete.

She spent, now, hours every day with him. Or he spent hours every day—all the time when he wasn't at school—with her. He sat by her bedside. He drew pictures for her. He told stories to her. He made her laugh. He made her tell him exactly what kind of pains she was feeling. He did everything he could think of to distract her from those pains. And more and more he tempted her to tell him about her almost totally consuming suspicion that she was being poisoned by Gerhard. By her husband. By his father. . . .

It was terrible even to consider the idea; but she couldn't help it. For if she did, she reasoned, the child might really be able to give her a grip on that rug to which she was clinging.

To give her a grip by dispelling her suspicions; and thereby help her to cast out the monster from her house, and start to reconstruct her life.

Yet still she couldn't bring herself to do it. And she might never even have approached the subject if she hadn't, one Sunday afternoon in July, received a visit.

Her visitor was David Chezzel.

She didn't want to see him, and she would have told him not to come if he had phoned first. But just as she had gone to him unannounced, so he came to her; and was shown into her bedroom by Gerhard.

'Fran dear, why didn't you let me know?' he gushed; and sitting down on the side of the bed, took her hand.

She had neither the strength nor the inclination to answer his question.

'How,' she muttered, 'is the book going?'

'Well. Fantastically.' He paused. 'You're not still thinking—?'

'No,' Fran said. 'No, of course not. I guess I was just clutching at straws before. Trying to find some explanation for the unexplainable.' She gave a tiny smile and suggested: 'Inexplicable?'

'Oh Fran,' David breathed. 'Do they really have no idea?'

'None.'

'I was sure you must be away—since I hadn't heard from you. But then I thought maybe I'd just call, and—Gerhard told me. I came right over.'

'That was sweet of you,' Fran said, as she wondered whether anyone had ever been so loathed as she was loathed by David. To be going through this pretence now, when he had known all along, or when, even, he had planned. . . . The rug lurched, and another piece was clawed from it. She hung on tighter, and told herself David is just writing a book. I am just suffering from a disease. David doesn't even loathe me. His gushing is natural to him. He might, possibly, like me, and be grateful for the help I have given him. Certainly there's *some* resentment in his feelings towards me, otherwise he *wouldn't* be writing that story. But such resentment is, as I have said time and time again, understandable. And resentment does not equal loathing.

'How's Cyrus?'

'Well. Very well. He's been so sweet I can't tell you.'

'I can imagine.' A pause. 'Talking of Cyrus, I was just saying to Gerhard—my sister's coming to New York next week for a few days with her three kids. It's a birthday treat for the twins. They're exactly the same age as Cyrus. I was thinking of giving a kind of children's party for them. Do you think Cyrus would like to come?'

I don't know about Cyrus, Fran wanted to say, but I know I wouldn't like him to. She said 'You'll have to ask him.'

Then she closed her eyes, and winced.

'I'm sorry, David,' she whispered. 'I'm very grateful for your visit. But would you mind going. I'm—' she winced once more.

'Of course not. I just wish I could do something.'

'Oh,' Fran said, as David stood up, and started to back away from her—and as she clasped her rug more tightly than ever—'you can. Just keep on writing. So I can have a really good book to read.' She winced yet again. 'What's happening to your poor heroine now?'

David stood there, looking at her. Then, in a voice as normal as hers, and with a little laugh, he said 'I'm afraid she's about to die.'

Fran was crying when Cyrus came into the room a little later. The effort of hanging on was too much for her. She didn't want to die, she sobbed to herself. And why should she die? She *wasn't* a bad woman; she was sure. She had always loved those near to her, she had helped those whom she could help, and while she had always wanted power over people she had never, as far as she was aware, misused her power. So why, why, why? Even as a representative of the rich, of the leaders, of the tyrants, as David liked to called them—as one of the editors, publishers, writers of a certain version of reality—she didn't think she was particularly worthy of blame. Aside from the fact that not only she, but David himself, she was equally sure, would have found any alternative version far less acceptable—or even worse—than the one she had always supported. So why, why—

Why, her son asked her, was she crying.

Because, she wept, holding the boy—and letting the final few strands of her magic carpet fall away beneath her (she would, she told herself, be able to grasp them again later)—because—she hesitated, still unable to say what she thought, but equally unable not, at last, to say something—'Because I'm afraid I'm going to die, and I don't want to.'

Cyrus stared at her. 'You're not going to die,' he told her. 'You can't die.' Then: 'Why are you going to die?'

'Because,' Fran said, 'David has written a story about me. And he has written that I'm going to die.'

Even in her present state she could tell how absurd she sounded. . . .

She rushed on, 'Sometimes poets and writers see things before they happen.'

But as she was saying this, Cyrus himself had started talking. And when she heard his words Fran realized he didn't find her absurd at all.

'Why,' the child asked, 'did he write something like that?'

Oh, Fran thought, I am lost. . . .

'Because,' she whispered, 'he hates me.'

'But *why*?' her son insisted.

'Because,' Fran said yet again, trying to think of some way of putting it so that Cyrus would understand, 'he thinks that

I have written a book in which he plays the part of a clown.'
She stopped for a second. 'No, not of a clown. Of a dog. And
he doesn't want to. And so—' but she could keep it up no
longer. And falling back on her pillows, and almost screaming
with pain, she just cried 'Oh Cyrus, I'm sorry.'

Cyrus, however, ignored her apology. He looked thoughtful,
and shook his head. 'I don't understand,' he murmured, 'why
David invited me to a party next week if he hates you.'

'He doesn't hate *you*,' Fran whispered. Then, before either
falling asleep, or losing consciousness, she added, 'But you don't
have to go if you don't want to. Even if you said you would.'

Cyrus had said he would; and in spite of what his mother had
told him, five days later, he went.

Fran would have been mystified if she had thought about
it much; but by the day of the children's party she couldn't
think about anything much any more; apart from her pains,
the fact that she was going to die, and the reason for this fact.
She heard Gerhard tell her that he was going to take Cyrus
over to David's; the words registered; and then she fell back
into the burning mist that was enveloping her.

She had believed, when she had let those last shreds of
reason slip, that she would be able to recover them. She wasn't
able to. She *was* being poisoned by her husband. He was clearly
using a poison that was unidentifiable, untraceable; and she
was going to die. Gerhard was going to inherit all her money—
it was too late to change her will—and then was either going
or not going to marry Lucie Schmidt. She didn't know, and
it didn't matter any more. There was nothing but chaos in
the world, and madness. Madness, hatred and death. She
repeated these words over and over again. Madness, hatred
and death. Madness, hatred and death. They became a chant,
echoing and resounding in her head. Madness, hatr . . .—she

started to laugh. She was being written out of existence. She was dying. . . .

She called for the nurse who had been with her, at Gerhard's insistence, for the last few days. (Few weeks? She wasn't sure.) The woman came rushing in. Fran felt herself being given an injection. She clung to the white uniform. Her parents were in the room. She reached out for them. She was aware of someone making a telephone call. She heard Gerhard's name being mentioned. She didn't want to see him. She closed her eyes. He was there. He was saying 'Fran, Fran.' He was holding her. She said 'Cyrus, I want Cyrus.'

'I left him at David's,' Gerhard whispered. Shouted? 'I thought it would be better. I'd only just arrived when your father called. I came straight back. But I thought it would be better,' he repeated, 'if Cyrus stayed there.'

'Cyrus,' Fran shrieked—though she heard no sound leave her lips. 'I want to see Cyrus. You've got to get him back.' She started hitting at her husband. She punched. She fell back. She tried to get up again. The pains were destroying her. She couldn't move. There were waves breaking over her, pulling her out to sea. No, she tried to scream, I don't want to die. I don't—The sea was ablaze, and she was falling into the flames. They reached up to her body. They reached up to her mouth. They reached into her brain. No! she tried to scream. No!

Some time later she was aware of Cyrus kissing her, and whispering something into her ear. Then, after a final effort to save herself, she lay still, and was silent.

She had no idea, when she awoke, whether it was night or day, or for how long she had been unconscious. All she was aware of was that Gerhard, Cyrus and her mother were gazing at her and smiling; and that she no longer felt any pains. She could feel where they had been—it was as if she had a bruise in her stomach, or had had something torn from her—but the pains themselves were gone. She smiled, very weakly, back at the faces looking down on her, asked for a glass of water—and then promptly fell into a deep, dreamless sleep.

A week later she was able to get out of bed; and three weeks after that she was strong enough to leave, with Gerhard, for a month in Vermont; to do nothing but rest, read, and convalesce.

Till then no one, least of all her, had spoken much of her sickness; other than to say that whatever had afflicted her had reached a climax the afternoon of David's party, that everyone had been terrified she was going to die, but that though she had been in a coma for four days, after that climax had passed she had started, very slowly, to pull through; and the doctors had announced she was going to recover. They still had no idea what had been wrong; but guessed it had been some virus that had burned itself out—or been burnt out by her own desire to live.

Sitting in the New England sun, however, in front of the small white house in the hills that Gerhard had rented, Fran thought it was time to talk more openly of what had happened.

She started, therefore, by apologizing to Gerhard for her behaviour.

'You know,' she said with a smile one afternoon, 'I really did think you were trying to poison me. I fought against the idea, but—' she shrugged, 'I did.'

Gerhard looked embarrassed. 'I know,' he murmured, his head lowered. 'But you were sick, weren't you?'

'I'm sorry, anyway,' Fran said—as it occurred to her that when she had finally given up the fight against the madness of that notion, she had both had her great crisis—and started to recover from it.

'But in a way,' she continued a little later, 'it's done me good. It's as if'—she paused, searched for the right image, and then found it—'I were in a zoo, with a wild animal that was kept locked up in a cage. As long as it was locked up it scared me so much I became obsessed with it. So much so that I couldn't see anything in the world apart from that animal. But finally I had the strength to release it—or didn't have the strength to keep it in its cage—and somehow—well, I don't know whether I fought it and beat it, or whether I realized that though it was wild, and even dangerous, as long as I wasn't scared of it—it wouldn't hurt me.'

Gerhard smiled, and took her hand. 'Anyway,' he said, 'it's all over now. And when you're completely better we can go back to New York, and everything will be as it was before.'

Fran lay back in her chair, and wondered. Possibly, she told herself. But she doubted it. Now that that animal was out in the open—and now, too, that she had seen it was possible to fall through space and survive—she doubted that anything would be the same as before. Strangely, however, the idea exhilarated her. . . .

'Except for one thing.' Gerhard added. And lowering his head again, he told her that his affair with Lucie Schmidt was over. . . . He had broken with her, he said; or to be honest, she had broken with him. She had gone back to France, and was getting married again.

Fran stared at her husband for a while, wondering what to say. Then, realizing there was nothing to be said, she merely touched his blond hair with her finger tips—and quietly, gratefully, changed the subject.

'Do you think,' she asked, 'I should apologize to David?'

Gerhard looked up, and also seemed grateful. Then he said 'No. Why? You didn't accuse him of trying to poison you, did you?'

'No,' Fran murmured—hesitantly.

'Well then. Besides, I've been thinking about David and

142

that book of his, and you were right. He really shouldn't have started it, considering everything you've done for him.'

Fran shrugged. 'It doesn't matter now.' She smiled. 'Just as long as it's a good book. Have you heard from him?'

'No. I called him a couple of times, to thank him for sending Cyrus home in a cab, and to let him know how you were, but there was no reply. And since then I've sort of forgotten about him.'

'Poor David,' Fran said, as she wondered, very calmly now, whether Gerhard had indeed been poisoning her, and had lost his nerve—or Lucie?—at the last minute. She supposed it was quite possible. Anything was possible. Though she doubted that he would ever try again, even if he had. He had made his point, and she had taken note of it. Taken note of it to such an extent, in fact, that she would, she decided, as soon as she got back to New York, put half her money in his name, without any strings attached. Which might not make him feel entirely free; but would at least be a start. . . .

'There is one thing I must do though.'

'Which is?'

'Apologize to Cyrus.'

Gerhard laughed. 'What did you accuse Cyrus of?'

'Oh, nothing. But that day, after David had come round, I wanted to talk to him. But as I obviously couldn't tell him I suspected you of trying to poison me, I told him I was dying because David had written that I would.'

'Just because of that?'

'Yes.'

'Well I don't know about apologizing. But you'd better explain. Otherwise Cyrus might grow up thinking people can be killed by the stroke of a pen.'

'Yes,' Fran repeated, more thoughtfully this time. 'I didn't really mean it like that of course. I—I didn't really mean anything. It was all just a story. But—I'll talk to him as soon as we get home.'

She did; and Cyrus, who had been staying with his grand-parents while his mother and father had been in Vermont, listened to her in silence.

'Oh sure,' he said, when Fran had finished her explanation, 'I realized you were only telling me that because you were sick. I mean that would be dumb, wouldn't it?' He smiled at her, and then looked slightly defiant. 'But I'll tell *you* some-thing. I thought it was so mean of David to hate you, and that was such a mean story he was writing about you, that when I went round to that party that afternoon, I went into his study and found the notebook where he was writing it. Then I tore all the pages into little pieces and threw them out of the window.'

Fran stared at him. 'You didn't,' she whispered.

'I did.'

'Oh but that's terrible.'

'He shouldn't have written it.'

'But—did you tell your father?'

'No. I haven't told anyone.' Cyrus shrugged. 'Apart from you, when I got back from the party. But I guess you didn't hear me. You were unconscious.'

'No,' Fran murmured, 'I guess I didn't. Or maybe,' she added, feeling suddenly faint, 'I did. In fact I think I probably must have. But,' she concluded, still staring at her son, 'you shouldn't have done it, Cy. It really was a terrible thing to do.'

Cyrus looked crestfallen now; and sounded disappointed as he asked, 'Do you think David will forgive me?'

'Yes,' Fran said, kissing the child. 'Yes,' she repeated, 'I'm sure he will.' Then she closed her eyes and whispered, feeling more faint than ever, 'It'll be me he'll never forgive.'

144

Nor, she thought later that day, sitting alone in her living room, should he. For she realized not only how David would interpret this whole affair, but how she at last interpreted it. Oh it was still quite possible that Gerhard had been trying to kill her, and had lost his nerve; or, more poetically, that having faced the beast of unreason, she had overcome it. But somehow neither of these explanations, in the light of what Cyrus had revealed, really satisfied her any longer. They neither of them went far enough. Now she saw the events of the past few months in a different fashion. She saw them, she told herself, as a parable of oppression; as an illustration of the power of tyrants. She had indeed supported David in order to control him. When he had attacked her, to free himself from her grasp—she had sickened. When she had attempted, and failed, to bring him to heel—she had grown worse. And if, when it was nearly too late, she hadn't turned to Cyrus and used him, albeit unconsciously, as her ultimate weapon, she would have died. As it was she had reasserted her power; she had won; and she had survived. Obviously she was glad to have survived; and while she had chided him, she would always be grateful to her son for having saved her. But, she thought—at what a cost. To have to spend the rest of her days with the knowledge that, however much she had now renounced her longing for control, she had already done irreparable damage; and worse, with the knowledge that when and if she met David again, the overwhelming hatred with which he would then greet her would make his former feelings seem almost like affection.

In fact she did meet David again; though not before eighteen months had passed. Yet strangely—wonderfully—when she did, it wasn't at all with hatred that he greeted her. . . .

She bumped into him outside the Museum of Modern Art; and would have avoided him if she had seen him coming. But the writer, who was with a friend, was so changed that not till the last moment—just before he stopped, and said 'Hi Fran'—did she even recognize him. And if the friendliness of his tone took her aback, his appearance shocked her far more. It wasn't that his once luxuriant black hair was now cut very short and flecked, in spite of his comparative youth, with grey. Nor that while before he had been soft and tending to plumpness, he was now so thin as to be gaunt; almost emaciated. It wasn't even that his expression was no longer the expression of a pleading spaniel, or that his mouth no longer seemed about to utter some self-condemnation. No, what really shook Fran, really staggered her, was that while she had found him repellent before—now she found him beautiful. Not good-looking, in the way that Gerhard was; nor exotic, in the way that other young men she knew were. But—beautiful. In the way that deserts were beautiful. Or bare winter trees.

To begin with, after she had taken all this in, and after she had told herself that she had never, in her whole life, seen anyone so transformed, Fran was tempted to reply with a muttered 'Hi', and to rush on; if only because she was afraid that she was going to be confronted with something—with the cause of that transformation?—still more appalling than the hatred she had expected to see. But before she could do so David had asked her, in a quiet spare voice, how she was; and she, despite her fears, had forced herself to meet his eyes. And once she had she couldn't have rushed on if she'd wanted to. For what she saw there was not only not hatred, but something that seemed the very opposite of hatred; and something that, in any case, transfixed her.

'I'm very well,' she said gently; 'and you?'

David nodded, and smiled. 'Yes. I am too.' Then he looked away, as if embarrassed by her gaze; and went on to say how sorry he was to have left the apartment like that, without a word, and that he did hope she had recovered the keys from the people next door, and that everything had been in order, and that—

Yes, Fran interrupted. Yes of course, and she had understood. Of course she had understood. And she too had been so sorry. . . .

Looking down at her shoes, she asked David where he'd been living.

'I've been fortunate,' the man said. 'I was lent a house in the country in Italy by some friends. I was there for almost a year. Then I went to England and rented a cottage in Sussex for six months. I got back to New York three weeks ago.'

'And'—this very quietly—'you're still writing?'

Another nod. 'Yes. I started—something different.'

Then they were both silent for a while; until Fran, almost whispering, said 'What's it about?'

Their eyes met once more.

David shrugged. 'Basically,' he said, 'it's the story of a writer who is supported by a rich patroness whom he believes, mistakenly or otherwise, is a criminal; or at least a member of the criminal classes. Hating her for the compromise with crime that he feels her patronage represents, he writes a story in which she dies. Poisoned by his hatred, the woman actually does start to die. But then, at the last moment, her child destroys the manuscript of the story; and she starts to recover. The writer is so—' David hesitated—'stunned, I guess, by this evidence of the power of love, that he has a kind of breakdown, goes to Europe, for a while, and eventually comes to see that—' David hesitated again—'he might achieve more, both for himself and everyone else—and might also be happier—if he accepts the implications of what has happened, and learns a lesson from the child. Sure, it means he'll have to make compromises, but—' David stopped. 'I guess you could say that the moral of the piece is that it's better to be compromised and love than try not to be compromised and hate. But I don't know whether it is. I don't think in fact there's a moral at all. I think really—it's just a story about a group of fictional people who are doing their best to live. That's all.'

As he finished this account David blushed; and now seemed so embarrassed Fran had the feeling that *he* might rush off. But then he glanced at his waiting friend, who was studying the traffic on 53rd Street, and pulled himself together.

'I must be going,' he murmured.

'Yes,' Fran said—though hardly audibly—'so must I.'

Their eyes met one last time; and they held each other's gaze until David stepped forward, put his arms around her, and told her: 'Take care, Fran.'

For a moment, as she remembered the man's previous embraces, Fran hung back. But after that moment she relaxed; and feeling happier than she could ever remember feeling— happier, and more relieved—she whispered 'And you too.'

They stood there; two people who, though possibly enemies, had sealed a treaty of friendship. Then, promising only to see each other soon, they turned; and went their separate ways.